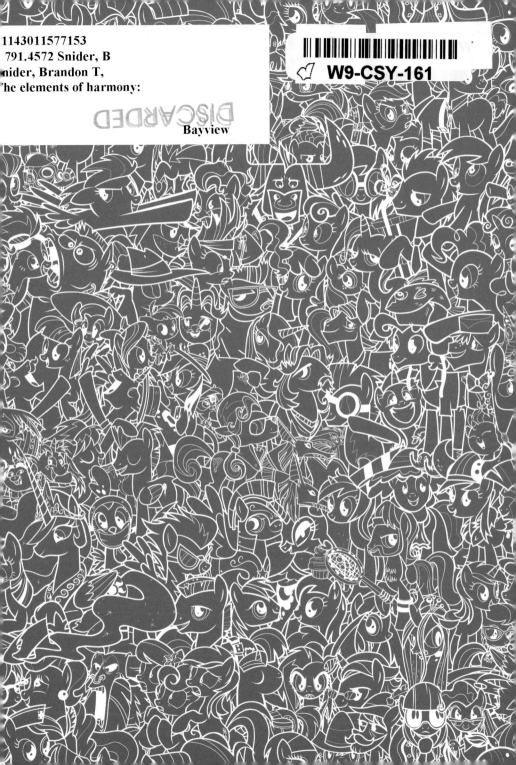

W9-CSY-161

The Story
of the Mane Six

Not too long ago...
In the magical land of Equestria...

A curious young pony named *Twilight Sparkle* discovered an ancient prophecy. It warned of a terrible, looming danger: Nightmare Moon.

Twilight Sparkle alerted Princess Celestia. The princess did not heed her apprentice's advice. Instead, she told the bookish pony she'd been spending too much time in the library.

Princess Celestia gave Twilight Sparkle two special missions. The first was to travel to Ponyville and check on the arrangements for the Summer Sun Celebration. The second mission was to make new friends!

Twilight Sparkle arrived in Ponyville and met a unique group of ponies.
Each one was especially suited to prepare for the festivities.

Applejack made yummy food while *Rainbow Dash* cleared the skies. *Rarity*
decorated the town in style while *Fluttershy* prepared harmonious music.

Pinkie Pie threw a surprise party welcoming Twilight Sparkle to Ponyville. It made Twilight Sparkle feel very special. Everything was going perfectly.

The Summer Sun Celebration was beginning, but Princess Celestia was nowhere to be found. Something was wrong.

The danger that Twilight Sparkle warned Celestia about had arrived. The ancient prophecy had come true. Nightmare Moon had appeared.

Nightmare Moon declared eternal night and plunged Equestria into darkness. There was only one thing that could defeat her and save Equestria: *the Elements of Harmony*!

Twlight Sparkle and her new friends left to find the five known
Elements: loyalty, honesty, generosity, laughter, and kindness.
The sixth Element was a mystery.

They used their unique strengths to defeat obstacles deep in the
Everfree Forest. Soon they retrieved the Elements and faced their enemy.

Uniting the power of the Elements, the ponies defeated Nightmare Moon, changing her back into Princess Celestia's younger sister, Princess Luna.

The two sisters reconciled their differences and Equestria was saved. During the battle, Twilight Sparkle had discovered the mysterious sixth Element: *magic!*

Twilight Sparkle's new companions made her so happy. Princess Celestia noticed. She decided to give the young pony a brand-new mission.

Twilight Sparkle was to remain in Ponyville and continue studying the Magic of Friendship. And that is how the brave group of ponies became known as the Mane Six.

The ELEMENTS OF harmony
Volume II

The Official Guidebook

Brandon T. Snider
with Natasha Levinger

LITTLE, BROWN AND COMPANY

New York Boston

Little, Brown and Company
Hachette Book Group
1290 Avenue of the Americas, New York, NY 10104
Visit us at lb-kids.com
mylittlepony.com

First Edition: June 2017

Little, Brown and Company is a division of Hachette Book Group, Inc.
The Little, Brown name and logo are trademarks of Hachette Book Group, Inc.

Library of Congress Control Number 2013000609

ISBNs: 978-0-316-43197-2 (hardcover), 978-0-316-43196-5 (ebook)

Printed in the United States of America

WOR

10 9 8 7 6 5 4 3 2 1

Contents

1

THE MANE SIX AND SPIKE

TWILIGHT SPARKLE

THE ELEMENT OF MAGIC

From the moment she entered Celestia's School for Gifted Unicorns, Twilight Sparkle *knew* she was destined for greatness. Within her soul was an insatiable thirst for knowledge. She read every book she could get her hooves on! Her research paid off when Princess Celestia gave this diligent pony the most important mission of her life: study the Magic of Friendship and absorb its valuable lessons. Twilight Sparkle set out on a life of adventure, facing dangers and challenges at every turn! Thankfully, she had her powerful pony pals backing her up when she needed them the most. After discovering the truth behind the mysterious Elements of Harmony, Twilight Sparkle elevated from simple ponyhood to become an Alicorn and the ultimate Princess of Friendship. From the Castle of Friendship, and together with her five best friends and Spike, Twilight Sparkle continues to protect Equestria from threats while learning about herself and spreading joy along the way.

Twilight Sparkle is now an ALICORN. That means she's a pony who has Pegasus wings *and* a horn.

Her parents are Twilight Velvet and Night Light!

TIMELINE

Receives her cutie mark through the study of magic!

Officially becomes Princess Celestia's apprentice.

Moves from Canterlot to the Golden Oak Library in Ponyville.

Becomes an Alicorn!

Twilight Sparkle elevates to the Princess of Friendship!

Begins training Starlight Glimmer.

RAINBOW DASH

THE ELEMENT OF LOYALTY ⚡

Make way for Rainbow Dash! No, seriously, get out of the way—**RAINBOW DASH IS COMING THROUGH!** As the number-one flier in all Equestria, Rainbow Dash rules the skies as the Pegasus pony supreme. Without *her*, who'd make sure the weather was awesome all the time? But Rainbow Dash's skills weren't always astounding. Learning to focus on her strengths and not her weaknesses took a while. With the help of her friends, as well as her fellow Wonderbolts, Rainbow Dash is as competitive and self-confident as ever. Got an aerial challenge? She's ready for it! She'll even throw in a dollop of sass for good measure.

PEGASUS PONIES have wings that they use to fly. They can also control the weather and walk among the clouds.

TIMELINE

Carries the Cloudsdale flag in the Equestria Games opening ceremony.

Receives her cutie mark and completes her first Sonic Rainboom!

Meets her favorite author, A. K. Yearling, and helps her with a Daring Do book.

Joins the Wonderbolts!

Trains her friends for the big buckball game against Appleloosa.

THE ELEMENT OF LAUGHTER

Need a power-packed dose of peppy positivity? Pinkie Pie has everypony covered! Her giggle is infectious and so is her unstoppable spirit. Anypony who hangs around her long enough is bound to get caught up in her infectious spirit. When she's not slinging sugar at Sugarcube Corner, she's planning parties for all her besties. Who doesn't love parties? Pinkie is also an excellent talker with the gift of gab. Speaking of gifts, she loves to give them! What else is she supposed to do with that big heart? Pinkie loves having friends but is extra

 thankful to be included in such a wonderful group of inspiring young ponies. Hooray for friendship!

Her full name is Pinkamena Diane Pie.

TIMELINE

Throws her first surprise party and attains cutie mark.

Gets a job at Sugarcube Corner in Ponyville working in the Sweet Shoppe.

Invents the party cannon!

Makes friends with the Yaks of Yakistan

Faces off against Cheese Sandwich in an epic party-planning contest.

APPLEJACK

THE ELEMENT OF HONESTY

Lookin' for a pony who tells it like it is? Applejack's yer gal! Some fillies can't handle the truth, but don't worry your pretty little head. She might be blunt, but she's also as sweet as pie (when she wants to be). Whether family or friend, Applejack has your back! She'll work her hooves till they're sore and, at the end of the day, still devote time to her best friends. *That's* loyalty. Just don't make her do girly stuff—it's not her favorite. Despite a stubborn streak, Applejack has learned a lot over the years, including the real value of honesty. That's what a regular pony might call maturity, but Applejack calls it good ol'-fashioned *learnin'*.

Applejack is an EARTH PONY, which means she has a unique connection with nature and the great outdoors.

TIMELINE

The Apple family opens a farm and orchard known as Sweet Apple Acres.

Moves to Manehattan and lives with her aunt and uncle Orange for a short time.

Applejack meets Twilight Sparkle and invites her to brunch.

Organizes the Apple family reunion!

Reunites with her fillyhood friend RaRa/Countess Coloratura.

THE ELEMENT OF GENEROSITY

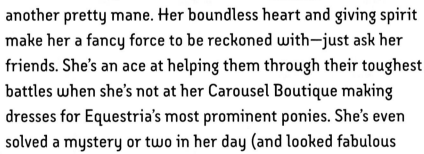

Glamour! Style! Sophistication! At first glance, one might assume a polished pony who commands the room would be superficial and shallow. That's not the case with Rarity. She's not just another pretty mane. Her boundless heart and giving spirit make her a fancy force to be reckoned with—just ask her friends. She's an ace at helping them through their toughest battles when she's not at her Carousel Boutique making dresses for Equestria's most prominent ponies. She's even solved a mystery or two in her day (and looked fabulous doing it!). It hasn't been easy balancing her career as a fashion designer with her mentorship of younger ponies. Regardless, a perfectionist like Rarity always finds a way to make it work.

Rarity is a UNICORN. They've got horns and can perform magical feats!

TIMELINE

Rarity is born in Ponyville.

Meets Twilight Sparkle for the first time and gives her a makeover.

Rarity takes top prize in Manehattan Fashion Week.

Receives a rainbow spool of thread from Miss Pommel.

The Canterlot Carousel opens!

FLUTTERSHY

THE ELEMENT OF KINDNESS

When her pony pals are down in the dumps, Fluttershy swoops in to cheer them up in her own sweet and quiet way. She delights in the beauty of friendship and the nice feelings that come from being nice. Fluttershy is definitely a little bit meek, but she can be fierce when she needs to be. She's faced her fears and grown a whole bunch, and she continues to build her self-confidence! Oh, and she loves her animals. **A LOT!** Even when they're being naughty little critters. She's probably the most in tune with creatures of the forest of all the ponies she calls her friends.

She's been transformed into a vampire fruit bat-pony hybrid nicknamed Flutterbat.

TIMELINE

Fluttershy is born in Cloudsdale.

Discovers her ability to communicate with animals and receives cutie mark.

Makes an unlikely friend in Discord.

Joins a singing group known as the Pony Tones!

Goes to Las Pegasus and stays at Gladmane's resort.

SPIKE TAKES OVER!

Need a helping hand, a quick delivery, or friendly smile? There's a passionate little Dragon named **SPIKE** who can do all three (and then some). He's a handy pal to have around when trouble rears its ugly head. But Spike wasn't always so confident and self-assured. A sensitive and playful spirit, he's grown in leaps and bounds since arriving in Equestria. His journey began as a mysterious egg that young Twilight Sparkle hatched during her time at Celestia's School for Gifted Unicorns. After a bit of enchanted chaos, Celestia witnessed something very special: A bond had formed between her favorite student and the baby Dragon. The two became fast friends and grew even closer over time. Spike eventually became Twilight's faithful assistant and traveled with her to Ponyville. Together with their new friends, Spike and Twilight discovered the Magic of Friendship.

Spike loved hanging out with the Mane Six but took a *liking* to Rarity. He had a total crush

I love gems! A LOT.

I can play the piano. And sing!

on her! Rarity considered Spike a supportive friend and her favorite Dragon. He even helped her out of a down period after her design for a puppet theater was met with a not-so-great response. However, Spike didn't inform Rarity that a spell meant to help had accidentally corrupted her. He was too afraid of losing her friendship. After breaking the spell, the two friends made up, and Rarity reminded Spike that he should never be afraid of telling the truth. It was a lesson he kept with him from that point onward.

My breath is magical fire.

As the only Dragon in a group of ponies, Spike often felt out of place. His friends poked fun at him for acting more like a pony than a Dragon. It made him question his identity and where he came from. He decided to investigate his origin and took off in a great Dragon migration, looking for answers. Spike soon found himself in the Dragonlands, competing in the Gauntlet of Fire to become the new Dragon Lord. It all happened so fast! After some hard-won teamwork, Spike realized that it's not *what* he is that's important. It's *who* he is that really matters, and that's a baby Dragon with a pony family.

I make the best nachos in Equestria. It's true!

SPIKE IS HUM DRUM!

Spike has a wild imagination. That's what comic books do to impressionable young Dragon minds. And it's awesome! Reading comic books allows Spike to travel across fantastic worlds filled with valiant superheroes and dastardly villains. Don't get him started on all the amazing superpowers—they're the best! Despite not having incredible super abilities, Spike is a hero in his own right. Whenever he doubted himself, he'd remember to be brave in the face of danger. If his friends were in trouble, Spike would break out of his shell and do the right thing, no matter the cost! Powers, schmowers. Once such instance found Spike and his pony pals transported to the fictional city of Maretropolis after a magic spell pulled them into a comic book. His friends became the city's protectors,

the **POWER PONIES**, and he became their sidekick, HUM DRUM! In the end, Spike realized that he didn't need fancy powers to be great friend.

Applejack is
MISTRESS MARE-VELOUS

Fluttershy is
SADDLE RAGER

Pinkie Pie is
FILI-SECOND

Rainbow Dash is **ZAPP**

Rarity is
RADIANCE

And Twilight Sparkle is
THE MASKED MATTER-HORN

EQUESTRIAN ROYALTY

From within her shimmering castle in Canterlot, **PRINCESS CELESTIA** rules Equestria with an attentive ear and an open heart. Celestia's mentorship to young ponies gives her the greatest hope for the future. She takes great pride in encouraging ponies to seek out new experiences in the pursuit of self-betterment. Twilight Sparkle, Celestia's most famous student, continues to impress the princess with her unwavering belief in the Magic of Friendship. Twilight's passion and positivity inspire Celestia to seek peaceful resolutions to Equestria's most troublesome issues. She recently used her leadership skills to improve the relationship between ponies and Changelings.

The princess commands a powerful magic that she uses to raise the sun each morning.

As the Equestrian sun lowers, the shining moon rises courtesy of **PRINCESS LUNA**, Princess Celestia's younger sister. The royal siblings have faced numerous hardships throughout history, with their bond growing stronger over time. Luna faced her greatest challenge during her transformation into the devious Nightmare Moon. With the help of Twilight Sparkle and the Elements of Harmony, Princess Luna was restored to her former self and hopes to stay that way. Luna prefers order and restraint, though her temper has been known to

flare. She's grateful that her sister and friends help guide her toward the light when darkness comes calling.

PRINCESS CADANCE, also known by her full name, Princess Mi Amore Cadenza, rules the Crystal Empire alongside her husband, Shining Armor. She's a patient and sympathetic leader, who uses her impressive magic to serve her subjects. Cadance developed such inspiring traits while studying with Princess Celestia when she was a filly. Now, as a mother to young Flurry Heart, Cadance's heart is full of love for both family and kingdom. Though royal life can grow wearisome for Cadance, she continues to seek the thrill of adventure in her spare time.

Princess Cadance was once Twilight Sparkle's foal-sitter.

SHINING ARMOR is Twilight Sparkle's older brother, Princess Cadance's husband, and Flurry Heart's father. He's also the captain of the Canterlot Royal Guard. With so many important titles, it's no wonder he's an inspiration to many of his loyal subjects. Though he appreciates their adoration, his wife and child command his attention the most. Shining Armor is devoted to his family and seeks to protect them at any cost.

When the Crystal Heart broke, winter overtook the city.

FLURRY HEART's birth was something new in Equestria—an Alicorn pony had never been born before. To mark the occasion, a traditional Crystalling ceremony was announced. The Crystal Heart would instill the powers of light and love within the small foal. But Flurry Heart's uncontrollable magic made such a ceremony difficult. Only by banding together were the ponies of the Crystal Empire able to restore the Crystal Heart and save the royal baby.

THE CRYSTALLING CEREMONY

Whenever a new pony is born in the Crystal Empire, the parents present the foal in front of the Crystal Heart, an ancient artifact at the center of the Empire. Then everypony shares the joy and love they feel at that moment,

increasing the Crystal Heart's power and helping the entire Empire. Without the warmth of the Crystal Heart, the Crystal Empire would be buried under a mountain of ice and snow, and lost once more.

FAMILY MATTERS

THE APPLE FAMILY

If it wasn't for **THE APPLE FAMILY**, Ponyville wouldn't exist! They're the ponies who founded it way back in the day. The Apples wandered around Equestria, snatching up seeds wherever they could find them. They were hoping to settle down someplace nice but hadn't found a place to do it. As a kindness, Princess Celestia gave the Apples a patch of land near the Everfree Forest, where Granny Smith found the very first zap apple.

She started making her famous zap apple jam, and soon enough, ponies from all over were stopping by to scoop up some. Sweet Apple Acres was born and has been the heart of Ponyville ever since.

GRANNY SMITH has seen and done just about everything there is to see and do! As the grande dame of the family, she's been telling tales and sharing wisdom for a *long time*. Ask about her days as a high diver. She might show off a move or two. Though her memory can be foggy, Granny Smith always has a mouthful of zingers at the ready.

HAYSEEED TURNIP TRUCK is the helper of the family. He's ready to tackle any job he's given, even if he doesn't know how to do it! While he's not the shiniest apple in the bunch, he's got spirit and gusto to spare.

BIG MCINTOSH, aka **BIG MAC**, is a pony of few words. He prefers working hard to chattering on and on. When he's not plowing fields, you might find him playing Oubliettes and Ogres.

AUNTIE APPLESAUCE is even older than Granny Smith, if you can believe it! Has anypony seen her teeth?

BRAEBURN is happy to show anypony around Appleloosa. He's helpful like that. If you ask nicely, he might even strum on his guitar for you.

AUNT ORANGE and **UNCLE ORANGE** are Applejack's family that live in Manehattan. They're city ponies who giggle at good ol' country folk. But that's okay. They're still family just the same.

27

THE PIE FAMILY

When it comes to mining, **THE PIE FAMILY** rocks! Need a stone? They've got a farm full of the biggest boulders and smallest pebbles around. Harvesting rocks is what they do, and they love every minute of it. Stop by for some gravel and hear the story of Holder's Boulder. It's a good-luck boulder their ancestor Holder Cobblestone found in a Dragon's nest. There's a rumor going around that the Pie Family and the Apple Family *might* be related, but that wouldn't change anything about how the families feel about one another—they may have some different traditions, but they're already super close.

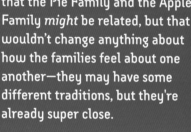

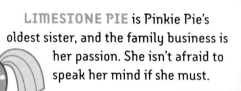

LIMESTONE PIE is Pinkie Pie's oldest sister, and the family business is her passion. She isn't afraid to speak her mind if she must.

MAUD PIE is Pinkie Pie's older sister. She might seem aloof at first, but get to know her and she's kind-hearted as Pinkie Pie.

MARBLE PIE is Pinkie Pie's baby sister and the demure pony of the family. She prefers to let her older siblings do all the talking.

IGNEOUS ROCK PIE and **CLOUDY QUARTZ**, also known as Pa and Ma Pie, were arranged to be married by a Pairing Stone. They're proud rock farmers and even prouder parents.

THE SHY FAMILY

THE SHY FAMILY lives in Cloudsdale. It's where **MRS. SHY** spends her time gardening and **MR. SHY** collects clouds since retiring from the weather factory. The heroism of their daughter, FLUTTERSHY, makes them burst with pride! Their son, ZEPHYR BREEZE, dropped out of mane therapy school. He *never* leaves the house. Mr. and Mrs. Shy wish he'd get a job *and* his own place.

THE CAKE FAMILY

THE CAKE FAMILY owns Sugarcube Corner, where they make the most delicious baked goods in Ponyville. CARROT CAKE and his dear wife, CUP CAKE, are hard-working business owners who delight in making treats for all types of events. That is, when they're not chasing their twin foals, POUND CAKE and PUMPKIN CAKE.

PONY PALS & ANIMAL ALLIES

PONY PALS

Deep within the Everfree Forest lives **ZECORA**, a wise, almost mystical Zebra. Need something? She has potions and spells for all occasions from revealing hidden magic to recovering your voice. Don't be frightened by her unusual ways—Zecora is a friend to all ponies. Stop on by, and she'll tell you a rhyme!

SEABREEZE is a magical sprite known as a Breezie. He can be plainspoken at times, but he's not trying to be rude: The dimness of his fellow Breezies can get frustrating! With the help of new friends like Fluttershy, Seabreeze has learned how to be more patient and kinder when it comes to his family.

THE SMOOZE is a glowing, green slime creature and one of Discord's pals. When he's not causing ponies to gasp in fright, he's gobbling jewels and leaving an icky trail of slime wherever he goes.

PRINCE RUTHERFORD is a gruff Yak leader who sought to improve relations between Yakyakistan and Equestria. He can be a blowhard when he doesn't get his way and is known for his tantrums. The cordial ponies of Equestria welcomed him with open hooves, showing him the power of friendship.

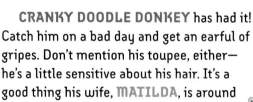

CRANKY DOODLE DONKEY has had it! Catch him on a bad day and get an earful of gripes. Don't mention his toupee, either— he's a little sensitive about his hair. It's a good thing his wife, MATILDA, is around to even out his temper. She's a Donkey damsel with a heart of gold, who always tries her best to lift her sweetheart's spirits.

ANIMAL ALLIES

ANGEL is Fluttershy's bossy bunny. He thinks he can get away with just about anything since he's a lovable little puff of cuteness. Guess what? He's right! Despite his consistent naughtiness, Angel's heart is kind and pure (for the most part).

CONSTANCE loves to sing! She's a bird. It's her thing. Sometimes her songs are so beautiful they make Fluttershy tear up. Too emotional, right?

For a toothless little alligator, **GUMMY** has bite! He prefers chilling out with Pinkie Pie. His other hobbies including lying around, remaining silent, and staring. He's an odd, little reptilian sidekick.

HARRY is a hugger. He's bursting with love and affection! As one of Fluttershy's animal pals, this bear is a master of the embrace. Got a cave and some free time? Harry gives snuggle lessons.

Rarity's cat, **OPALESCENCE**, does whatever she wants. Most days she's too tired to care. Get too close and she might even hiss! Despite her catitude, Rarity loves her cuteness nonetheless.

OWLOWISCIOUS is Twilight Sparkle's faithful fowl companion. He's an observant pet who's always looking out for his master and her friends. Owlowiscious is the strong, silent type, but when it comes to Spike's absentmindedness, he definitely gives a hoot.

PEE WEE is a lil' baby Phoenix who hatched from an egg found by Spike. He enjoys hanging out with Spike and eating ice cream. One day, he hopes to grow up, burst into flames, and be reborn anew!

PHILOMENA is Princess Celestia's majestic Phoenix. The mystical bird might *look* feeble and featherless, but give her some time. Soon a brand-new creature will emerge in a burst of fire! No big deal.

TANK the tortoise goes at his own pace and doesn't apologize for doing things his own way. He prefers a relaxing atmosphere when he's not competing for attention. If only Rainbow Dash, would let him hibernate!

When Applejack calls, faithful **WINONA** comes loping over. She's a helpful herder who's all about pleasing her master. When she's not delivering important messages, Winona enjoys a nice, long grooming.

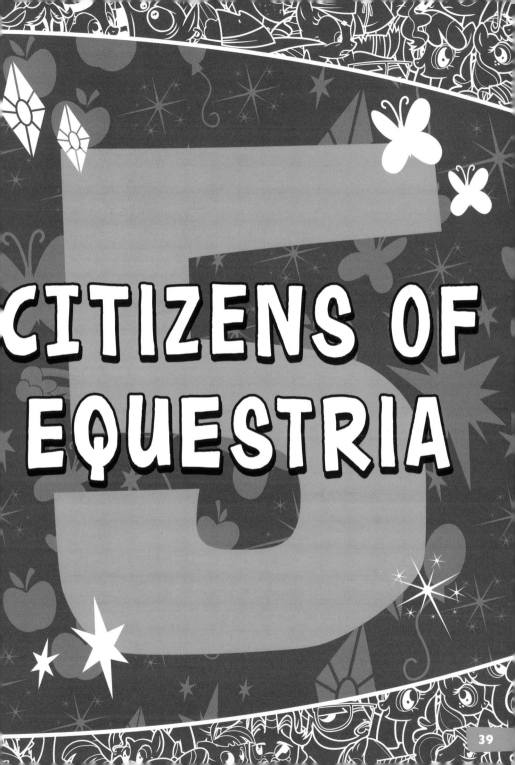

5 CITIZENS OF EQUESTRIA

CUTIE MARK CRUSADERS

Everypony is on a journey, but it's difficult for young ponies to be patient. All Apple Bloom, Scootaloo, and Sweetie Belle wanted to do was figure out who they were and what they were destined to do. They were desperate to discover their hidden talents, hoping a cutie mark  would reveal itself and change their lives forever. Instead of worrying about it alone, they came together to form the ultimate support team: **THE CUTIE MARK CRUSADERS**. After a series of trials, the Crusaders successfully acquired their cutie marks and set out to prove their worth. Receiving a cutie mark doesn't mean they're done figuring everything out, of course. It simply means they're energized and on the right path. These feisty fillies are passionate about helping other young foals figure out their paths.

GABBY is a mail Griffon and honorary Cutie Mark Crusader—she can't get a cutie mark of her own, so her friends hoofmade custom mail clips with the Crusader mark for her!

BABS SEED is Apple Bloom's cousin and the founding member of the Crusaders' Manehattan branch.

APPLE BLOOM is ready to blossom! As Applejack's little filly sister, Apple Bloom knows what it's like to feel overshadowed. She comes from a big family of farmers who work day and night to provide for one another. Apple Bloom loved her life but dreamed of something bigger. Once she joined up with her fellow Crusaders, she took the lead and learned to shine. Apple Bloom's fearlessness and determination make her a force to be reckoned with even when the odds are stacked against her.

Cute little **SWEETIE BELLE** is a good-natured filly who tries hard but doesn't always hit the mark. Despite her frustration, she never gives up! Having Rarity as a big sister can make a pony like Sweetie Belle kind of insecure. Becoming a Crusader made Sweetie realize that she could be anypony she wants to be. Competition is good sometimes, but not when it prevents a pony from fulfilling their destiny.

SCOOTALOO doesn't like standing around listening to somepony blather on about the past. She's too excited for the present! Scootaloo's passion makes her an anxious sort who sometimes acts before thinking. *It happens.* Her fellow Crusaders are quick to remind her to focus her to on the tasks at hoof. Scootaloo has skills, too! She's a musical maestro, a masterful mechanic, and the head of the Rainbow Dash Fan Club.

SCHOOL-AGE PONIES

DIAMOND TIARA likes only the finest of things. She enjoys poking fun at ponies she thinks are lacking and behind the times. *Rude*. Someday she'll learn that putting ponies down won't make her feel better about herself.

SILVER SPOON leads a privileged life. She's been given everything she could possible want. Sometimes she wonders if it'll ever be enough. In the meantime, she'll just keep on buying things she doesn't need.

PIPSQUEAK is president of his class at the Ponyville Schoolhouse. It's an honor he always dreamed of achieving. The Cutie Mark Crusaders helped him run a fierce election campaign. Pip sure has come a long way since his early days in Trottingham. Go, Pip, go!

TWIST puts the *cutie* in *cutie mark*. Her sweet confectionery skills earned her a candy cane heart, which she puts to good use making sugary treats.

SNIPS and **SNAILS** are pony pals with a bit of a naughty streak. Impish Snails is balanced out by happy-go-lucky Snails. Together, they're quite a pair!

FEATHERWEIGHT is editor in chief of the *Foal Free Press* newspaper and a staunch investigative reporter (in his own mind). Need a copy of the paper? He's got a million. No, seriously—please take one.

SUNNY DAZE and **PEACHY PIE** are best friends who do *everything* together. They're super lovable to boot. When they're not reciting poems while roller-skating, they're sharing a basket of piping-hot curly fries. *Mmmmmm*, curly fries.

RUMBLE dreams of being a fast flier like his older brother, Thunderlane. He's a determined colt with a ton of heart. Keep an eye on the skies!

TENDER TAPS is a dancing machine who's hoping for a big break. He's shy about his talents, but once he gets his hooves moving, there's no stopping him.

ZIPPORWHILL is such a fan of the Pony Tones that she got them to play at her cute-ceañera. She's also a huge fan of puppies and kitties, but then again, *who isn't?*

THE WONDERBOLTS

Look, up in the sky! It's the Wonderbolts! In ancient times, Princess Celestia needed a team of Earth ponies, Unicorns, and Pegasi to help protect Equestria from harm, so she assembled a brave battalion of plucky ponies picked from the E.U.P. Guard of Protective Pony Platoons. As their numbers grew, Celestia drafted General Firefly to select the best fliers in all the land for an all-star team called the Wonderbolts! Together, these ponies perform death-defying aerial stunts, delighting audiences across Equestria.

Young ponies with the skill, ambition, and heart are encouraged to apply to the Wonderbolts Academy, where they'll learn all the tricks of the trade and even a few surprises.

SPITFIRE is team captain and the academy drill instructor. She tells ponies what they're doing *wrong* but also what they're doing *right*. Spitfire makes her team work. She's not always nice about it. In her opinion, that's the only way her students will ever learn.

LIGHTING DUST is a highly competitive flyer and Rainbow Dash's good friend. She flies recklessly, and doesn't always see how her actions will affect other ponies. She might have an even bigger ego about her flying than Rainbow Dash, and was actually removed from her leadership role in the Wonderbolts because of it.

BULK BICEPS is a huge pony with tiny wings, but he can fly with the best of them. He's a new cadet at the Academy, but he's also represented Ponyville in the Equestria Games relay, been a masseuse at the La Ti Da Spa in Ponyville, and even taught foals how to lift heavy things. He's afraid of butterflies.

VAPOR TRAIL is a soft-spoken young Pegasus who starts her Wonderbolts trial week helping her best friend, Sky Stinger, perform his tricks...at the cost of her own flying ability. She learns that being a Wonderbolt really *is* important to her, and dedicates herself to improving her own flying, earning a spot at the Academy.

SKY STINGER is a new recruit at Wonderbolts Academy. Brash and arrogant, he was sure he would be a shoo-in for the program. When it turned out that his best friend, Vapor Trail, was secretly helping him, his confidence was shattered, and they had a brief falling-out. Ultimately, he practiced his flying and become a cadet!

TEAM MEMBERS

MISTY FLY never passes up a chance to show off for her fans and admirers. And she definitely has plenty of both. She's not one to boast, but in her opinion, she's the 'bolt to beat.

HIGH WINDS thinks life is a total breeze. Her nickname is Hoof-in-Mouth, which is pretty fair.

SURPRISE is always appearing out of nowhere! It's off-putting. Her nickname is Slowpoke—but what's in a name anyway?

FLEETFOOT wants to be good *so bad*. To her, flying can be really serious stuff, so she studies all the cool moves every chance she gets. She loves watching and listening to great fliers for tips.

BLAZE doesn't worry about much. She's a sleek sky torpedo after all. On a good day, no one can catch her as she zooms across the sky—most days are good days.

SOARIN' balances work and play. Life is too short not to have some fun along the way. When Soarin' isn't flying high, he's looking around for his next piece of pie. He is one chill pony.

WIND RIDER will go to any length to protect his legacy—even if it means lying! He's a disgraced former Wonderbolt who framed Rainbow Dash after she broke his aerial record. Somepony needs to take the wind out of his sails.

THE BEST OF THE REST

SUNBURST is a Unicorn, and was Starlight Glimmer's best friend when they were young ponies. He's great at magic, and when the new baby Alicorn Flurry Heart and the Crystal Heart needed someone to step up, Sunburst was the pony to do it. Now he's the royal crystaller to Flurry Heart.

CHEESE SANDWICH is a superduper party pony (his words), and gives Pinkie Pie a run for her party-planning money. He even has a *bigger* party cannon than Pinkie, and once won a "goof-off" with her. Cheese Sandwich has some seriously cheesy skills.

SAPPHIRE SHORES is a big star, known across Equestria as "the Pony of Pop." She had Rarity design quite a few outfits for her over many moons, including a whole gem-based wardrobe for her Sapphire Shores's Zigfilly Follies tour.

CORIANDER CUMIN and **SAFFRON MASALA** are the father and daughter owners of the Tasty Treat, a restaurant that serves exotic cuisine in Canterlot. Their passion for cooking brings them through every obstacle—including picky food critics.

MISS POMMEL is a talented seamstress. Rarity's generosity inspires her to quit her job with Suri Polomare, a cruel and scheming Manehattan designer, and branch out on her own.

MOONDANCER was one of Twilight Sparkle's earliest friends, but after Twilight blew off her party, she turned into a recluse, giving up on friendship entirely. She's since come around, thanks to Twilight's heartfelt apology, and has a load of friends!

QUIBBLE PANTS is a fellow Daring Do super fan who is *absolutely sure* which A. K. Yearling books are the very best. No argument will change Quibble's mind! Over time, though, he and Rainbow Dash realize ponies can love things for very different reasons, and that's okay.

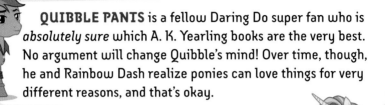

SASSY SADDLES runs Rarity's Carousel Boutique in Canterlot. Initially, she butted heads with the fabulous designer, but has come to embrace Rarity's vision of personalized care and love in every outfit. Under Sassy, the store is a huge hit.

COUNTESS COLORATURA is one of Equestria's hottest pop stars. Unfortunately, she let fame go to her head and acted like a diva until her childhood friend Applejack revealed the error of her ways.

DARING DO, also known as **A. K. YEARLING**, is the title character and author of the Daring Do books. She sometimes attends the Daring Do Conventions as her author alter ego as a cover for new daring adventures.

TREE HUGGER is a member of the Equestrian Society for the Preservation of Rare Creatures, and was Fluttershy's guest to the Grand Galloping Gala. She likes nature just as much as Fluttershy. Their friendship initially makes Discord incredibly jealous, but they all become friends.

MALEVOLENT MISCHIEF-MAKERS

QUEEN CHRYSALIS was once Changeling royalty, until her quest to acquire the power of love corrupted her spirit. Then she desired one thing—revenge on the ponies who kept her from her ultimate prize— even as Twilight Sparkle tried to befriend her and show her how to lead her people with love.

LORD TIREK is a cruel Centaur who tried to steal Equestrian magic after escaping from his prison in the dark realm of Tartarus. His boiling anger and frightening appearance are enough to make anypony shiver with fear. Thankfully, Twilight Sparkle and her friends defeated Lord Tirek, sending him back to his underworld prison.

AHUIZOTL is an intimidating and devious creature with a taste for thievery! He's gone toe-to-hoof with Daring Do a time or two—since she's his archenemy. When backed into a corner, Ahuizotl commands his gang of jungle cats to strike! He's not very nice. He's not very nice *at all*.

DR. CABALLERON and his henchponies will do anything for money. Got something that needs stealing? He'll do the job. Caballeron has a taste for ancient artifacts. Watch out for his entrancing accent—it's been known to get ponies in trouble.

SURI POLOMARE is a fashion maven with a feisty temper. If she's in a mood, get out of her way! The process of creation stresses her out. When Suri doesn't get what she wants, she snaps. That's what happens when a pony's ego goes bonkers.

SVENGALLOP is Countess Coloratura's scheming former manager. Nopony is fooled by his flashy flair and wily words anymore. It's clear he's totally out for himself. If Svengallop says he'll make a pony a star, tell that pony to pick up her hooves and hightail it.

GLADMANE once owned the Las Pegasus resort where he pit his employees against one another for sport. A bad boss like that deserves the boot! And that's exactly what Gladmane got. Now he's at home doing the high-roller hustle all by himself.

GARBLE is a rude teen Dragon who's got a beef with Spike. Is Garble jealous that Spike has the best friends ever? Probably. Or perhaps Garble just needs a big ol' hug. Try giving him one, but be careful of his nasty fire breath.

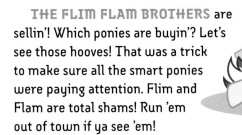

THE FLIM FLAM BROTHERS are sellin'! Which ponies are buyin'? Let's see those hooves! That was a trick to make sure all the smart ponies were paying attention. Flim and Flam are total shams! Run 'em out of town if ya see 'em!

SILVER SHILL was been a tricky pony in the past, helping con ponies Flim and Flam sell their bogus healing tonics to unsuspecting ponies by pretending to be an eager customer. Silver Shill has turned a new leaf, and now thinks honest is *usually* the best policy.

ZESTY GOURMAND is one of Canterlot's most esteemed food critics and the creator of the three-hoof rating system. The city's elite dine only at restaurants the distinguished Unicorn reviews, meaning that without her stamp of approval, some restaurants can really struggle. A firm believer that fine cuisine must have subtle flavors, Zesty is a tastemaker with very specific tastes.

7 REFORMED RASCALS

STARLIGHT GLIMMER

The story of **STARLIGHT GLIMMER** is one of transformation. It begins with her founding a small village on the outskirts of Equestria where cutie marks weren't just frowned upon—they were forbidden! She believed that ponies sharing their special talents with the world led to disharmony. Using a fake magic stick called the **STAFF OF SAMENESS,** Starlight removed the cutie marks of everyone in the village and replaced them with boring equals signs. When Twilight Sparkle and friends arrived, they couldn't believe their eyes. They challenged Starlight's leadership, exposing her as a fraud to her followers. After a fantastic adventure through time, Starlight Glimmer realized the error of her ways. She learned that uniqueness *is* important. Starlight was at a crossroads. She was desperate to change for the better and make up for her numerous wrongdoings. Twilight Sparkle reached out with the opportunity of a lifetime. She took on Starlight as a pupil and began teaching her the Magic of Friendship.

Starlight Glimmer took up residence in the **CASTLE OF FRIENDSHIP** and began her training. Thus far, she's reconnected with her old friend Sunburst, built trust with her *new* friend Trixie, and defeated a changeling invasion. It's a start! Though she's not the best magician in Equestria, she's learning how to spell-cast like a pro.

As a spirit of chaos, **DISCORD** the Draconequus made Equestria a wretched place for ponies. He was imprisoned in stone for his crimes and later broke free to cause trouble again. But once he experienced the true power of friendship, Discord was changed for the better. He might not be perfect, but he's trying his best and that's all anypony can hope for!

TRIXIE is a magician whose jealousy of Twilight Sparkle made her mean and vengeful. Or was it her lack of real magical skills that made her that way? *Hmmmmmm.* Trixie eventually loosened up, making amends with her former rival. Now she tries her best to be a good pony...for the most part.

GILDA the Griffon used to think she was the prankmaster general until she got a taste of her own medicine, courtesy of Rainbow Dash. Is Gilda bitter? Maybe. But she's learned her lesson and is trying to be a better friend than enemy.

AROUND EQUESTRIA...

DRAGONS

DRAGONS are mystical, flying lizard beasts that come in many different sizes, shapes, and colors. They have magical fire breath and spend their time munching on gems when they're not looking for a nice cave to take a nap in. While younger Dragons like Spike are sweet, others can be temperamental. Some are downright evil, like **DRAGON LORD TORCH**. He's the father of **PRINCESS EMBER**, who now serves as a kinder, gentler Dragon Lord.

GRAMPA GRUFF is an ornery old Griffon who longs for the days of yore! That's before his homeland of Griffonstone was so run-down. Life was tough back in the day, but he liked it! *Oh, how he loved it.* Nowadays, he just sits around waiting for outsiders to stop by so he can take advantage of them. What a greedy-pants. If only his granddaughter, Gilda, could talk some sense into him.

GRETA might come off as a grouchy Griffon at first, but give her some space. She's simply cautious around new friends. Offer a scone and get to know her. She might just follow.

GABBY

GILDA

BREEZIES are a group of enchanted pixies who ride the winds of Equestria in large swarms, carrying pollen. Their home is a secluded hollow that can be reached only by traveling through a magic portal. The Breezies speak their own bizarre language. They understand pony talk, but don't expect them to speak it. Breezies do *what* they want *when* they want, *okay*?

The **TRI-HORNED BUNYIP** is a sea-dwelling creature that lives in the deep water near Seaward Shoals, and speaks only in growls. Be careful when it surfaces—its mass has been known to cause tidal waves and flip ships. Its favorite food is a nice cucumber sandwich.

VAMPIRE FRUIT BATS are a terrifying nuisance that can suck an orchard dry in between flaps of their wings. Applejack was smart to build them a sanctuary where they can feed without ruining Sweet Apple Acres.

CIPACTLI is a cranky crocodile with a toad body. No wonder he's so snappy.

TWITTERMITES are little pests shoot lightning at unsuspecting ponies. When they're by themselves they're mostly harmless, but watch out when they swarm! The larger the swarm, the larger the lightning.

The **TATZLWURM** is a slithering, wormlike monster that lives deep under the ground. That's a good thing considering it has black mouth tentacles that it uses to guzzle its victims. Its sneeze is also diseased! Welcome to yuck city.

What's a cross between a panda and a bumblebee? A **BUGBEAR**, of course! He's majorly annoying despite the buzz in town. Don't get too close or he'll sting!

SLINGTAILS live in the Dragonlands and use their powerful spiky tails to hurl massive boulders at Dragons. Normally that would be a bad idea for any creature, but the Dragons like to use slingtails in their Gauntlet of Fire obstacle course.

STAR SPIDERS are scary. Especially when they nest in the corner of your room and, at night, after you've gone to sleep, crawl all over your face for fun.

Beware **TANTABUS** the phantasm! This strange smoke creature invades a pony's dreams and feasts on their power until they become nightmares. The more he eats, the stronger he gets, and the stronger he gets, the closer he gets to escaping into the real world. *Hmmmm.* Maybe don't go to sleep?

EQUESTRIA

Welcome to **EQUESTRIA**, where the Fire of Friendship burns bright for all to see! The story begins many moons ago, when three tribes of ponies used their unique skills to build a thriving society. Despite their ability to work in unison, Pegasi, Earth ponies, and Unicorns lived separate lives and often argued over their differing roles in the community. Then a terrible blizzard caused a food shortage, and the ponies were forced to seek out new lands, where they could resettle in peace. After finding a location that suited their needs, the tribes bickered over which group should control it. Their arguing created negative energy, empowering a group of evil beasts called Windigos. They were the ones who'd created the blizzard that caused the ponies so much trouble. When the three tribes began working together, it sparked the mythical Fire of Friendship, causing the Windigos to run away in defeat. When the dust settled, everypony came together in harmony to build their brand-new home into a beacon of hope that would be known far and wide as Equestria.

Come on down to APPLELOOSA for some homespun fun. Have a relaxing beverage at the Salt Block saloon or take a scenic horse-drawn carriage ride through downtown. It's a Western town that welcomes ponies of kinds. Come visit for a spell!

BREEZIE VILLAGE is a tiny town filled with magical sprites! It sits comfortably atop a series of mushrooms, surrounding a pond that can only be reached through a special portal.

Nestled high atop a mountain in the middle of the kingdom is **CANTERLOT**, Equestria's capital and home to the royal family. Its shimmering towers and radiant waterfalls serve as a beautiful welcome for visiting ponies of all kinds. The city is known for its high-society affairs and exciting events such as the Grand Galloping Gala, when ponies

gather to celebrate Canterlot's wondrous majesty. The city also plays host to Celestia's School for Gifted Unicorns, where ponies are taught the skills they'll need to become good citizens and careful magic wielders.

Look up! Gaze upon the billowing wonder of **CLOUDSDALE**, home to the flying Pegasi. It's also where the Weather Factory creates clouds, snowflakes, raindrops, and other assorted weather conditions. And it's home to the Wonderbolts Academy, where ponies learn to soar!

The historic and mysterious **CRYSTAL EMPIRE** was once one of Equestria's biggest secrets. Now the translucent domain is well-known for its culture and its famous Crystal ponies.

The **DRAGONLANDS** are a series of volcanic islands that play host to the many Dragons and Phoenixes of Equestria. Look to the skies and be wary of migrating Dragons. They're a fiery sort.

The **EVERFREE FOREST** is curious place, located at the far reaches of Ponyville. Tread carefully when entering. Dangers known and unknown

lurk beneath its leafy canopy. Timberwolves and Manticores roam freely, plants grow with wild abandon, and the weather has a mind of its own.

The FLAME GEYSER SWAMP is a foggy bog where fire can erupt from the ground without a moment's notice. A pony must be wary while passing through. Watch out for Chimeras!

GRIFFONSTONE is located in the Hyperborean Mountains, which lie to Equestria's east, this is the hometown of Gilda, Gabby, Greta, Grampa Gruff, and other Griffons. It is also known as the Griffon Kingdom

Looking to have an unforgettable weekend? **LAS PEGASUS** is the place to go! It's a lively town with something for everypony. You may never want to leave.

MANEHATTAN is the place to be for a pony who wants to take their career to the next level. It's a city that never rests, playing home to Equestria's movers and shakers.

PONYVILLE is a lively town filled with diligent and business-minded ponies from a variety of different backgrounds. Take a trip through the town marketplace, and a pony can find everything from baked goods to fashion and more! Ponyville was founded by a group of Earth ponies and has become a thriving community for art and commerce. Once the weather becomes warm, it's time for the Summer Sun Celebration, when ponies come together to throw one of the biggest parties in Equestria.

RAINBOW FALLS is famous for its marvelous and brightly colored waterfalls. The village is also known for its annual Traders Exchange, where ponies come to sell and trade rare items. High-flying ponies use the town's training course to help improve their skills for the Equestria Games.

SEAWARD SHOALS is a quaint coastal town where ponies who visit for the weekend often end up staying much longer. Its hilly vistas and casual atmosphere can make even an anxious pony relax.

The **SMOKEY MOUNTAINS** host two of Equestria's most famous families: the Hooffields and the McColts. Between its towering peaks is a thriving valley filled with playful creatures of all sorts.

The dark realm known as **TARTARUS** contains the vilest creatures imaginable. It's there that ancient beasts suffer for their evil deeds, doomed for all eternity.

With its spacious camping area and gorgeous rainbow waterfalls, **WINSOME FALLS** is where ponies spend time away from the hubbub of daily life.

RARITY'S FASHION EMIPIRE

"Welcome to the **CAROUSEL BOUTIQUE,** where every garment is chic, unique, and magnifique." Rarity's first and primary shop is located in her hometown of Ponyville, and has gotten rave reviews from both her clients and the esteemed *Clothes Horse* magazine.

Rarity opened the **CANTERLOT CAROUSEL**, a second branch of the Carousel Boutique, this time venturing out to the Canterlot market,

after designing for the famous Sapphire Shores on her Equestria-wide tour. This shop is run by Sassy Saddles, who has proven herself more than capable of running the store and making Rarity proud.

RARITY FOR YOU, the third shop in Rarity's growing dress-and-fashion empire, is located in glamorous Manehattan. The store almost opened to disaster, but all Rarity's best friends were able to come together and make the opening—and the shop—a huge success.

TALES FROM EQUESTRIA

EPISODE GUIDE
SEASONS 4, 5 & 6

Season 4

Princess Twilight Sparkle has become an Alicorn, but is having some trouble adjusting to her new role. Meanwhile, she and her best friends search for keys to open a mysterious chest. Twilight becomes the Princess of Friendship.

Season 5

The Princess of Friendship gets a castle of her own, and her friends discover a Cutie Map in her library, which shows them friendship problems across Equestria only they can solve. The group meets Starlight Glimmer, a special Unicorn with special issues.

Season 6

The arrival of Princess Flurry Heart—the first Alicorn birth Equestria has ever seen—brings Twilight Sparkle and the rest of the Mane Six to the Crystal Empire, and from there they explore more of Equestria at the behest of the Cutie Map. Back in Ponyville, the Cutie Mark Crusaders get their cutie marks and dedicate themselves to their calling.

Princess Twilight Sparkle: Part 1

Princess Twilight is having a hard time adjusting to the changes in her life now that she is an Alicorn. Princess Celestia has given her an important job at the upcoming Summer Sun Celebration in Canterlot, but her friends are leaving for Ponyville to prepare for the celebration back home. Twilight starts to worry that being a princess is only going to tear her and her friends apart. But she is soon distracted from her concerns when danger strikes: Princesses Celestia and Luna have gone missing, and the Everfree Forest is growing uncontrollably! Twilight knows that she must gather her friends to fight this evil and get the Everfree Forest back in order.

Their first stop is to confront Discord, but he claims his innocence and tells them to talk to Zecora. Zecora in turn tells them that even *she* doesn't know why the forest is acting the way it is. She says the only thing she has that can help is a potion that only an Alicorn can use. If Twilight drinks it, she can see what is troubling the forest.

Twilight takes the potion and is immediately transported in front of two thrones. Princess Luna walks out from behind one throne, but Celestia is nowhere to be found. Twilight asks her what is going on. Luna is clearly enraged and tells her that she will not be overshadowed by Celestia anymore. There will only be *one* princess! And it will be *Luna*. Luna then raises the moon in front of the sun, causing a solar eclipse. As this eclipse covers her completely, Luna transforms into Nightmare Moon. She laughs maniacally as Twilight looks on, terrified about the events she has just witnessed.

Princess Twilight Sparkle: Part 2

Still under the spell of the potion Zecora gave her, Twilight goes further back in time and witnesses Celestia using the Elements of Harmony to send her sister, as Nightmare Moon, to the moon's surface. Twilight goes *even further* into the past and sees a tree of crystal that Celestia and Luna refer to as the Tree of Harmony. Celestia tells Luna that the Elements of Harmony are the only way to defeat Discord and free Equestria. Twilight wakes up from the potion's magic and realizes that the reason the Everfree Forest is in trouble is because the Tree of Harmony is in danger!

Back in the present, she rushes to save her friends and the Tree of Harmony. But on the way Twilight is suddenly surrounded by gas-spewing plants. Spike finds their friends arguing in front of a dying Tree of Harmony. But Twilight's best friends rush back to rescue her, realizing they'd be lost without one another. When Twilight sees the black vines surrounding the Tree she remembers Celestia said the Elements of Harmony were the only way to save Equestria— so the only way to save the Tree of Harmony must be to give it the Elements.

Her friends are scared: What if they give up the elements and it doesn't work? The Elements are what keep them connected! Twilight reassures them: The Elements brought them together, but friendship will make sure they are never torn apart. They all agree, and Twilight gives the jewels to the Tree of Harmony. The vines disintegrate, freeing Princesses Celestia and Luna! Suddenly, a flower sprouts at the Tree of Harmony's trunk. It blooms and reveals a box with six locks. Celestia doesn't know where the keys are, but she does know it's a mystery Twilight won't be solving alone.

Friendship Lesson:

"[FRIENDSHIP IS] MORE IMPORTANT AND MORE POWERFUL THAN ANY MAGIC....FRIENDSHIPS MAY BE TESTED, BUT IT WILL NEVER *EVER* BE BROKEN!" —TWILIGHT SPARKLE

Castle-Mania

Princess Celestia suggests Twilight search the library in the Castle of the Two Sisters for more information about the chest from her most recent adventure. Twilight goes there, but can't find any new info on the chest! Back at Sweet Apple Acres, Rainbow Dash and Applejack are in a match to determine who is the "Most Daring" pony. So Applejack takes them to the castle because of an old legend Granny Smith told her about the "Pony of the Shadows" living there who possesses dark magic. Unbeknownst to them, Rarity has taken Fluttershy and Angel to the castle to find ancient tapestries to take back to the Carousel Boutique as inspiration. As they enter, a mysterious cloaked figure looms above the castle steps.

As the ponies spend more time in the castle, they get more and more petrified, finding trapdoors and the mysterious cloaked figure who seems to appear everywhere! Twilight reads about Celestia and Luna's favorite castle traps in their diary—including the "Organ to the Outside"—and then hears a pipe organ playing from somewhere beneath her. As the ponies grow more and more frantic, they all bump into one another. Twilight takes them to investigate the organ player and finds the cloaked figure there, playing the organ. She slowly pulls off the cloak to reveal Pinkie Pie! Of course Pinkie didn't mean any harm! She had followed Rarity and Fluttershy because she thought they were going to an "everypony-come-to-the-scary-old-castle-and-hide-from-each-other-while-I-play-the-organ" party.

Twilight doesn't learn anything new about the chest, but she tells her friends about a journal she found that Celestia and Luna kept when they were younger. She suggests they keep a journal together so they can share the lessons they learn.

Friendship Lesson:

"IT'S GOOD TO KNOW THAT WHENEVER YOUR IMAGINATION IS GETTING AWAY FROM YOU, A GOOD FRIEND CAN HELP YOU REIN IT IN....KNOWING SOMETHING ABOUT THE PAST MAKES IT EASIER TO DEAL WITH MY PROBLEMS IN THE PRESENT, EVEN THE SCARY ONES."
—TWILIGHT SPARKLE

Daring Don't

Rainbow Dash is counting down the seconds until the release of the newest book in the Daring Do series, which happens to be in three months and twenty-six days. When Twilight informs her the book release has actually been delayed Rainbow Dash goes into panic mode. She gets where A. K. Yearling, the author of the series, lives out of Twilight, and convinces her friends to go to the author's house to help her finish the book, as Yearling has obviously has gotten waylaid with distractions.

When they get there, they find her house in disarray! They are worried about A. K. Yearling's state of mind when she suddenly appears at the door and demands to know what

Rainbow Dash and her friends have done to her house! The Mane Six insist that they are innocent, and A. K. Yearling quickly scours her house for a book with gold binding and a horseshoe on the cover. She finds it and undoes a lock to uncover a golden ring, and quickly tucks it away. Suddenly, three stallions storm in and confront Yearling! She throws her coat and glasses at them and dons the garb of none other than...Daring Do!

And just like that, Daring Do is off on one of her amazing adventures. Rainbow Dash is desperate to help her stop the evil Ahuizotl, who had sent the three ponynapping stallions, but Daring Do is just as desperate to work alone. Rainbow Dash is never one to take no for an answer, though, and trails her hero from one escapade to another. But when her fanponying jeopardizes Daring Do's life, Rainbow Dash loses her confidence and tells her friends she is going to just give up and go home. This time her friends are the ones to never say no; they insist on helping Daring Do and proving to Rainbow Dash that she has it in her to be equal to her hero. In the end, they save Daring Do from danger *and* help Rainbow Dash's confidence. They all realize everypony needs help sometimes.

Friendship Lesson:

"NEVER UNDERESTIMATE THE POWER OF FRIENDS WHO'VE ALWAYS GOT YOUR BACK!" —RAINBOW DASH

Fight to the Finish

At the Schoolhouse, the Cutie Mark Crusaders learn about the upcoming Equestria Games contest. The class is split into teams, and Rainbow Dash will coach them. Whoever comes up with the best flag-carrying routine will get to carry the flag for the opening ceremony in the Crystal Empire! Their performances should show the judges what Ponyville means to them. Rainbow Dash will go with the winner of the contest in three days.

All the foals get to practicing as soon as they can. The Cutie Mark Crusaders will represent three races of Equestria all living together in harmony. Diamond Tiara and Silver Spoon bully them, but the Crusaders don't let it get to them.

Finally, they do their act for Rainbow Dash, and she loves it! Unfortunately, Diamond Tiara and Silver Spoon realize their only hope of winning is to sabotage the Crusaders. They take their bullying up a notch and dig in to Scootaloo for her inability to fly, meaning she shouldn't represent Pegasi in the routine. Scootloo's confidence nosedives, and Sweetie Belle and Apple Bloom also begin to lose confidence in her. Scootaloo gives up and decides not to compete.

On the way to the Games, Rainbow Dash finds out Scootaloo isn't going to compete, and hasn't even gotten on the train. She can't believe the other Crusaders let Scootaloo skip it! The fillies realize their mistake and return to Ponyville to remind Scootaloo that it's their differences that make them great! That's the whole point of their performance! Scootaloo is convinced, and with her friends by her side, they compete and do an amazing job, outshining the competition and earning the honor of carrying the Ponyville flag at the opening ceremonies of the Equestria Games.

Friendship Lesson:

"I THOUGHT I DIDN'T MATTER BECAUSE I'M DIFFERENT. THE THING IS, BEING DIFFERENT AND NOT BEING ABLE TO FLY AREN'T BAD THINGS. IT'S PART OF WHO I AM! PLUS, MY FRIENDS LOVE ME FOR THE PONY I AM NOW, NOT FOR THE PONY I COULD BE IN THE FUTURE. THAT'S REAL FRIENDSHIP." —SCOOTALOO

Power Ponies

Spike is obsessed with the Power Ponies comic book. While the Mane Six clean Celestia and Luna's old castle, Spike reads his favorite comic and comes across a part at the end telling him to join in on the adventure. When he reads that out loud he suddenly gets sucked into the book, along with Twilight Sparkle and all her best friends.

When Spike wakes up in Maretropolis he realizes his friends are now the Power Ponies, complete with awesome superpowers! When the ponies ask Spike what is going on, he tells them that they are living inside the comic book he was reading! The only way to get out is to defeat the villain known as the Mane-iac. Suddenly, she attacks them all and wins—the Power Ponies don't have much power against her. Just before she leaves the scene, the Mane-iac refers to Spike as Hum Drum, a powerless character in the book. Spike hates that he has no powers, even in his favorite comic book. It's not long before the Power Ponies once again find themselves battling the Mane-iac and her henchponies. She locks up the Power Ponies, but leaves Hum Drum behind because she considers him useless. This is a big mistake, however, because when Spike hears his friends singing his praises, it gives him the strength to persevere and mount a rescue attempt. After he neutralizes the Mane-iac's immobilization weapon and frees the Power Ponies, a pitched battle is fought, with daring heroics from everyone—including Spike. When he declares the Power Ponies victorious, they return to the castle and out of the pages of the comic book.

Twilight tells Spike how brave he was and how grateful she is for him saving them. He realizes he was strengthened by their friendship.

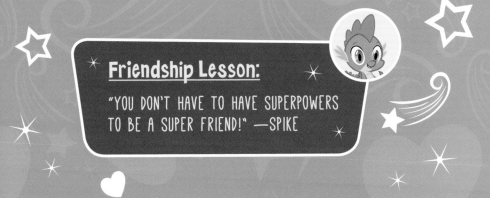

Friendship Lesson:

"YOU DON'T HAVE TO HAVE SUPERPOWERS TO BE A SUPER FRIEND!" —SPIKE

Bats!

Applejack is excited and ready to enjoy Applebucking Day when she suddenly realizes Sweet Apple Orchard is swarming with vampire fruit bats! Her number-one concern is keeping them away from her prized blue-ribbon apple— an apple that she plans to enter in a contest in Appleloosa. Fluttershy tries to help and has a word with the bats, but they won't get down. She suggests giving them their own sanctuary, but Applejack remembers Granny Smith's stories of a vampire fruit bat infestation and doesn't want to give them their own special place. Twilight suggests a spell that would take away the vampire fruit bats' desire for apples. All it would require would be Fluttershy's Stare to keep the bats in place while Twilight casts her spell. After some convincing, Fluttershy agrees—the spell works! The bats stay away from the apples after being Stared into submission by Fluttershy.

The next day, Applejack sees that her apples are all still being eaten! Twilight doesn't understand it. But later that evening, they discover a figure lurking in the shadows. It's Fluttershy, and she's turned into a vampire fruit bat-pony! She is now Flutterbat! When Twilight cast her spell on the vampire fruit bats, it transferred their desire to be vampire fruit bats to Fluttershy through her Stare. Twilight tells Applejack she thinks she has a solution, but they must use the giant blue-ribbon apple to do it. Applejack agrees, and they lure Flutterbat into a trap. She eats the apple and the rest of her friends surround her with mirrors, making her use the Stare on herself! Twilight casts the spell again and Fluttershy returns to normal.

After all the havoc that was created, Applejack agrees to Fluttershy's original plan of sectioning off parts of the orchard for just the vampire fruit bats. Later that night, as they have a laugh together, a tiny fang peeks through Fluttershy's mouth.

Friendship Lesson:

"YOU SHOULD NEVER LET ANYPONY PRESSURE YOU INTO DOIN' SOMETHING YOU DON'T THINK IS RIGHT. AND WHEN ONE OF YOUR CLOSEST FRIENDS TELLS YOU NO, YOU BETTER PONY UP AND ACCEPT IT, BECAUSE NOTHIN'S WORTH JEOPARDIZIN' A FRIENDSHIP." —APPLEJACK

Rarity Takes Manehattan

Rarity is excited about participating in Fashion Week and has taken her pony friends and Spike with her. She tells them that everyone is just so nice in Manehattan that it makes *her* feel extra generous! She then realizes she is late for her first appointment. She tries to catch a cab, but no one is showing generosity and are all fighting for their own cabs. Luckily, Rarity gets a ride to the Plaza.

Rarity joins her fellow designers. One of the designers is an old acquaintance, Suri Polomare, who likes Rarity's fabric and asks for a swatch. Of course, Rarity gives her a whole bolt. Rarity is quick to regret it, though, when she finds out Suri has created an entire line of dresses with Rarity's fabric and is passing it off as her own! Rarity tells her friends about the terrible situation, and, of course, they agree to help. Her friends work tirelessly for hours putting together Rarity's new line. They are not entirely happy about it since all their plans were canceled so they could help. When the work is finally finished, Rarity just takes the dresses and leaves without so much as a thank-you. She goes to the show and is quickly met with praise from the audience. But when she notices her friends aren't there, she realizes what she's done and leaves in tears to look for them.

After finding her friends, they tell her Suri said Rarity lost. Rarity doesn't care! All that matters is her friends are back. She tells them she arranged for a special showing of a musical just for them. At that moment, Suri's assistant, Miss Pommel, enters the theater. She gives Rarity the Fashion Week trophy, revealing Rarity *has* won! Suri lied because she thought she could win by default if Rarity was gone. Miss Pommel just couldn't lie any longer. She gives Rarity a rainbow-colored spool of thread as a thank-you gift for showing her that—even in the big city—generosity does exist. The spool of thread gives off a soft rainbow glow.

Friendship Lesson:

"I LEARNED THAT WHILE THERE ARE PONIES WHO WILL TAKE ADVANTAGE OF YOUR GENEROSITY, YOU SHOULD NEVER EVER LET THAT CAUSE YOU TO ABANDON YOUR GENEROUS SPIRIT. NOTHING FEELS WORSE THAN TAKING ADVANTAGE OF THE GIVING NATURE OF YOUR FRIENDS." —RARITY

Pinkie Apple Pie

Pinkie Pie is in the Golden Oak library with Twilight, who is studying genealogy. The idea of genealogy fascinates Pinkie Pie, who finds a scroll and quickly makes an amazing discovery! She runs over to Applejack's house and announces the fantastic fact—they are cousins! The whole family is very excited about the idea when Applejack notices that there's a smudge on the scroll, meaning they may not be related after all. Granny Smith says there's only one way to find out! They need to go on a road trip to visit their relative Goldie Delicious, who Granny Smith is sure will have the proof they need to show that Pinkie is related to the Apple family.

They embark on a difficult road trip. First the wagon

collapses. All the Apples start fighting until they remember they don't want to make a bad impression on their newest family member. But then Apple Bloom loses the map. How will they find their way now? They once again start to bicker but try to hide it, as they don't want Pinkie to regret being a member of their family. Granny Smith takes the lead, but the Apples are angry and upset. When they arrive at Goldie Delicious's house, they find a note saying she's running errands which gives the Apples time to apologize to Pinkie for being so argumentative and say they'd understand if she doesn't want to be a part of their family. Pinkie Pie doesn't know what they're talking about! They aren't just family; they're also best friends!

Goldie Delicious arrives, but unfortunately her family tree records are also smudged, so she can't really give an answer. Pinkie Pie is disappointed that she'll never know whether she's really an Apple. But the Apples tell her it doesn't matter to them whether they find their answer from a book, because they know Pinkie Pie is an Apple to the core!

Friendship Lesson:

"THROUGH THICK AND THIN, YOU'VE GOT YOUR KIN! I FEEL MIGHTY LUCKY, 'CAUSE SOME OF MY BEST FRIENDS ARE MY FAMILY. BUT WHAT MAKES ME A MITE LUCKIER THAN THAT IS THAT I'VE GOT SUCH GOOD FRIENDS, THEY FEEL LIKE FAMILY, TOO." —APPLEJACK

Rainbow Falls

Rainbow Dash is on her way to tryouts for the Equestria Games! She is very excited, despite not having the best team. She and her friends from Ponyville go to the tryout grounds and see the Wonderbolts: Spitfire, Soarin', and Fleetfoot, who are there to represent Cloudsdale, and even have their own cheering section. Rainbow Dash coaches her team and tries to instill confidence in them.

During a practice run, Soarin' clips his wing and goes into a tailspin. Rainbow Dash manages to save him before he hits the ground, but he's injured. Spitfire and Fleetfoot offer the vacant spot on the Wonderbolts to Rainbow Dash until Soarin' recovers. Rainbow Dash doesn't feel good about practicing with two teams at once, especially if one team doesn't know, but she ends up deciding to do it. Twilight finds out and Rainbow Dash assures her that it's just for practice so there's no harm. But just then, Spitfire and Fleetfoot come to tell her that Soarin' won't recover in time for the tryouts, and they offer her a permanent spot on the team. Rainbow Dash really wants to accept, but Twilight tells her to think about all the ponies she'll let down if she abandons the Ponyville team.

Rainbow Dash decides to fake an injury so nopony's feelings will be hurt. Her friends come to visit and feel so bad for her, they tell her if they win, she'll get all the medals. In the next hospital hospital bed, Soarin' tells Rainbow Dash he wishes he had friends like that. The truth is, he isn't really hurt, either—Fleetfoot and Spitfire are just worried that he'll hinder their performance. Rainbow Dash goes to confront them, and they are impressed with her loyalty. They tell her they could learn a lot from her, and they invite Soarin' back to their team. Both teams end up qualifying, and Rainbow Dash even gets a Wonderbolt pin from Spitfire that gives off a mysterious glow when she isn't looking.

Friendship Lesson:

"I LOVE TO WIN...REALLY, REALLY LOVE IT! BUT IF I EVER GOTTA CHOOSE BETWEEN WINNING AND BEING LOYAL TO MY FRIENDS...I'M ALWAYS GONNA CHOOSE MY FRIENDS. 'CAUSE AS MUCH AS I LOVE WINNING, I LOVE THEM WAAAY MORE!" —RAINBOW DASH

Three's a Crowd

Twilight is so excited because Princess Cadance is coming to visit! She's also a little anxious because their last visit was under very stressful conditions, but this time she has their day all planned out. They'll spend it at the Star Swirl the Bearded traveling museum, which happens to be in Ponyville for the day! Rarity, Pinkie Pie, Fluttershy, Rainbow Dash, and Applejack let her know they will do their best to make sure she has the best day ever with Cadance.

But right after Cadance and Twilight reunite, the whole group runs into Discord—who is blue and sneezing. He is just so very sick and asks the ponies to take care of him.

Everypony seems to have an excuse not to and just like that, he's Twilight's problem.

Cadance and Twilight agree to quickly help him, but typical of Discord, he puts them through a series of ridiculous requests that keep them tethered. Discord mentions there *is* a cure, a rare flower, but they'd all have to go look for it together. The trio travels by chariot, and Discord is left to rest while Twilight and Cadance begin the search. They end up finding this flower, but upon pulling it from the ground, a Tazlwurm emerges and attacks them! They manage to escape and bring the flower to Discord, but when they return, they find him completely healthy! Twilight is furious. He tells her he was testing her to see if they really were friends: Twilight always *says* she is his friend, but he doesn't think she's ever really shown it before. But now, giving up her time with Cadance to travel to the ends of Equestria just for him proves that she really is. And Cadance, for her part, actually enjoyed the adventure!

Friendship Lesson:

"WHEN YOU'RE WITH A GOOD FRIEND, EVEN THE MOST *CHAOTIC* DAY CAN WIND UP BEING A GREAT EXPERIENCE THAT BRINGS YOU CLOSER." —TWILIGHT SPARKLE

EPISODE 412

Pinkie Pride

Pinkie Pie is in party-planning mode since it's Rainbow Dash's birthday party! All the ponies agree there is no better party planner than her. But just as she makes a "Pinkie Party Promise" that this party will be the best one *ever*, a new pony appears. His name is Cheese Sandwich, and he declares himself to be Equestria's *premiere* party planner. Rainbow Dash proposes that Cheese and Pinkie work together to make *one* party. They both agree. Pinkie can't help but notice that everyone seems more excited about Cheese Sandwich's part of the party than hers.

Cheese Sandwich takes the lead and Pinkie Pie takes a backseat. Pinkie Pie starts to question her abilities and her identity. She decides to try some other jobs—surgery, mail delivery, and construction—but she's awful at them all. Back at her house, she sees all the pictures she has of parties she's planned that brought so much joy to so many ponies. With a renewed sense of energy, she is determined to show everypony that she is, in fact, "the bestest party pony around." She challenges Cheese to a "goof-off" and whoever wins will be recognized as the ultimate party-planning pony. He agrees, but Pinkie ultimately loses the challenge and decides to leave Ponyville forever.

Of course, her friends can't let her do that, and they rush to her side to apologize for treating her so poorly. She, in turn, apologizes for letting her pride get the best of her. What if she and Cheese really could work together? He appears and tells her he never meant to take her place; he just wanted to show her what a great party pony he was. The truth is, one day a long time ago, he came to Ponyville and saw Pinkie Pie's party skills, and ever since then he's been striving to be as good as she is! They work together to make a truly epic party. Before he leaves, he gives Boneless, his rubber chicken companion, to Pinkie Pie—which glows briefly.

Friendship Lesson:

"IF IT WAS A CHOICE BETWEEN FORFEITING A COMPETITION TO BE THE BESTEST PARTY PLANNER EVER OR GETTING TO HEAR MY FRIEND LAUGH AGAIN, I CHOOSE HEARING MY FRIEND LAUGH AGAIN, HOOVES DOWN!" —PINKIE PIE

Simple Ways

Rarity is announced as the pony of ceremonies for the upcoming Ponyville Days festival. She is very excited about all her plans, but she is most focused on making a good impression on the travel writer Trenderhoof. She has a *huge* crush on him. It is so huge that when he arrives Rarity can't even acknowledge him and hides behind Twilight's tail. When he does notice her, she faints. She manages to pull it together enough to show him around and see all the venues for the Ponyville Day festival events, but he doesn't seem very impressed. That is, until she takes him to Sweet Apple Acres and he is completely taken...with Applejack. He instantly declares her the pony of his dreams, which sends Rarity into a fit of despair.

Trenderhoof spends the rest of his time following Applejack around, but she is *not* into it—in fact, it makes her very uncomfortable. It gets worse when Rarity starts trying to get him away from her friend. She does whatever she can to get his attention: She dresses like Applejack, pretends to love apples like Applejack, plows fields, applebucks...she even takes on an accent like Applejack's! But nothing works. Rarity refuses to believe that Applejack doesn't like the attention, and is convinced that she is out to take Trenderhoof for herself.

Applejack tries to beat Rarity at her own game by acting like Rarity and showing up at a model scouting event she arranged, wearing a dress that the *real* Rarity might wear. Rarity splashes mud on Applejack's dress and that act makes her realize how far she's gone. She apologizes to Applejack and thanks her for snapping her out of her ridiculous state. Just then Trenderhoof appears, looking as if he were raised on a farm, and tells everypony he's moving to Ponyville! Rarity has a chance to use her newfound insight and convinces him that no one should change themselves just to impress somepony else.

Friendship Lesson:

"REAL FRIENDS WILL LIKE YOU FOR WHO YOU ARE, AND CHANGING YOURSELF TO IMPRESS THEM IS NO WAY TO MAKE NEW ONES. AND WHEN YOU ARE AS FABULOUS AS I AM...IT'S PRACTICALLY A CRIME." —RARITY

Filli Vanilli

At Fluttershy's cottage, her friends overhear her singing to her animals and remark how beautiful her voice is. They can't believe she doesn't use it more often. Rarity asks why she isn't a member of the Pony Tones like she is. They are even going to perform at Fluttershy's fund-raiser for the Ponyville Pet Center the next night. Of course Fluttershy could never do that because of her awful stage fright! They understand and agree on just helping set up the fund-raiser together.

The next morning they find out Big Mac has lost his voice and can't perform! Fluttershy is beside herself: What will happen to the fund-raiser? She decides to visit Zecora to see if she has a cure. Zecora can't help Big Mac, but she *can* give Fluttershy a brew of Poison Joke leaves that will deepen her voice and turn Fluttershy into "Flutterguy." Fluttershy is nervous about singing in front of everypony, but Rarity suggests not singing in *front* of everypony, but behind! That night she sings behind a curtain—with Big Mac miming his routine in front of the audience—and finds herself having a great time. She has *such* a great time that she agrees to perform with them again the next day. And once again, she has so much fun that she gets lost in the music, and she knocks down the curtain, exposing herself to the audience! Even though everypony is cheering, she can't handle the attention and leaves, crying.

Her friends follow her to help make her feel better. Rarity reminds Fluttershy of how much she loves to sing and what a good time she really had. Fluttershy thinks back on how much the crowd loved her and how much fun she had, and it makes her feel better. Fluttershy joins the Pony Tones for a performance in front of her friends and agrees to sing with the Pony Tones again someday.

Friendship Lesson:

"SOMETIMES BEING AFRAID CAN STOP YOU FROM DOING SOMETHING THAT YOU LOVE. BUT HIDING BEHIND THESE FEARS MEANS YOU'RE ONLY HIDING FROM YOUR TRUE SELF. IT'S MUCH BETTER TO FACE THOSE FEARS SO YOU CAN SHINE AND BE THE BEST PONY YOU CAN POSSIBLY BE!" —FLUTTERSHY

Twilight Time

The Cutie Mark Crusaders are learning new skills under Twilight's tutelage. They try very hard, but are not exactly succeeding. At school, they get frustrated as they watch Diamond Tiara and Silver Spoon let their money talk instead of their skills. But one thing the rich ponies don't have is constant access to Princess Twilight. When they beg the Crusaders to let them hang out with her, the Crusaders agree. Unfortunately, once the visit takes place, the rich foals fawn over Twilight so much she tells the Crusaders to leave their friends at home next time.

The next day the Crusaders find themselves the center of attention. Sweetie Belle and Scootaloo love their newfound popularity; Apple Bloom is unsure, but allows them to arrange a meeting at a restaurant with Twilight and have a few of their classmates watch her from a distance. It turns out the entire class has come to stalk her. Twilight is swarmed when she goes outside and answers questions from the star-struck crowd. The Crusaders gain even more popularity when their classmates hear that Twilight was only there because of the Crusaders.

At first the Crusaders revel in being popular ponies, but that night they quickly learn it has a dark side when they see Diamond Tiara keeping other colts and fillies out of a party. The Crusaders hightail it out of there and race to the Golden Oak Library, but other foals stop them at the door. Twilight is actually happy that so many colts and fillies in Ponyville want to learn from her, until Pipsqueak says that what he wants to learn is how to get popular by knowing a princess, like the Cutie Mark Crusaders have. Twilight is very disappointed in the Crusaders. They insist that they really do want to learn new things! The Crusaders apologize to Twilight for their mistake and go to leave, but their obvious remorse makes Twilight give them another chance. Before they leave their lesson, they make sure to disguise themselves so none of their classmates will recognize them.

Friendship Lesson:

"THE CUTIE MARK CRUSADERS TOOK ADVANTAGE OF TWILIGHT SPARKLE'S FAME SO WE COULD BECOME POPULAR AT SCHOOL. WE STARTED ACTING SPECIAL BECAUSE WE WERE FRIENDS WITH SOMEONE SPECIAL. BUT THEN WE LEARNED THAT FRIENDS ARE SPECIAL BECAUSE THEY'RE YOUR FRIENDS, NOT BECAUSE THEY'RE FAMOUS!" —SWEETIE BELLE

EPISODE 416

It Ain't Easy Being Breezies

Fluttershy gathers her best friends to tell them about the Breezies' upcoming migration through Ponyville. These tiny little creatures need as much encouragement as possible to get past Ponyville and back to their homes. When the moment arrives to watch them migrate through Ponyville, Spike accidentally lets a leaf fly in their way and they are unable to get back on track! Fluttershy comes to their rescue and brings them back to her cottage.

The Breezies are too scared to leave the nice safe haven

of Fluttershy's cottage. All except their leader, Seabreeze, that is. He is very angry about the delay. It seems any tiny thing stops them from going back home, and Seabreeze is getting more and more irate. He can't stand it anymore, and he makes a break for it on his own. He is unable to make any headway because of the heavy winds, and is soon attacked by bees! Luckily, Fluttershy saves him and Seabreeze is grateful. He tells her these kinds of dangers are exactly why he wants to leave Ponyville; he wants to get back to the safety of his own home. Fluttershy rushes home to get the other Breezies. It's time to go, and she tells them in no uncertain terms, even though it breaks her heart to have to do so that way (in a loud whisper).

Rainbow Dash can't make a breeze light enough to carry the Breezies home. Twilight remembers a spell that can help. She turns her friends into Breezies and all the ponies-as-Breezies help the actual Breezies home, guiding them and offering support along the hard journey. Before joining her friends to leave, Fluttershy bids the Breezies farewell and Seabreeze gives her a flower with a subtle magical glow.

Friendship Lesson:

"KINDNESS CAN TAKE MANY FORMS. SOMETIMES BEING TOO KIND CAN ACTUALLY KEEP A FRIEND FROM DOING WHAT THEY NEED TO DO. PUSHING THEM AWAY MAY SEEM CRUEL, BUT IT IS SOMETIMES THE KINDEST THING YOU CAN DO!" —FLUTTERSHY

Somepony to Watch Over Me

The Apples have decided that Apple Bloom is finally old enough to stay home alone and do the chores for the day while they run errands. She is so happy! She can't believe it! Before Applejack and Big Mac leave for the day, they give Apple Bloom the long list of chores. She eagerly accepts them and actually finishes quite quickly! But before she can enjoy it, Applejack, worried about her sister home alone, returns early and startles Apple Bloom, causing her to make a mess in the kitchen. When Apple Bloom tries to rectify it and instead makes it worse, Applejack decides it's too dangerous for Apple Bloom to stay home alone after all. Applejack is staying put!

Apple Bloom tries to convince Applejack that she can take care of things on her own, but Applejack hovers and won't stop overprotecting her sister. Desperate, Apple Bloom calls Sweetie Belle and Scootaloo over to figure out what to do. She decides to perform the errand that Applejack couldn't do because she came home to take care of her filly sister—delivering pies all the way across town. Scootaloo makes it look like Apple Bloom is sleeping, and when Applejack realizes that Apple Bloom is gone, she becomes distraught. What if she gets hurt out there, and Applejack never sees her again?

Applejack rushes to save her sister and does, in fact, find her in trouble. She is about to be attacked by a chimera before Applejack moves in and saves her. Apple Bloom realizes that she really does need her big sister sometimes, and Applejack realizes that even though she's upset that Apple Bloom snuck out, she still did a great job at home. While she will definitely still be in trouble for sneaking out, Applejack would totally trust her to be by herself again.

Friendship Lesson:

"BEING A BIG SISTER ISN'T A CHORE; IT'S AN HONOR.
BE CAREFUL NOT TO BE TOO OVERPROTECTIVE." —APPLEJACK

EPISODE 418

Maud Pie

Twilight Sparkle and her best friends gather at Sugarcube Corner, where Pinkie has them taste endless supplies of rock candy. Her sister Maud will soon be arriving, and it's their tradition to make and trade rock-candy necklaces! Pinkie wants to share that tradition with her friends since Maud is going away soon to get her "rocktorate" in rock science. She can't *wait* to see how well her best friends and her sister get along!

Maud arrives and sadly doesn't make the best impression with her lack of enthusiasm and her obsession with rocks. After an unsuccessful day of trying to get along, they all go home to regroup. They do want to give Maud a fair chance, so each of the ponies to share their interests with Maud, but their connections fall flat. In a last-ditch effort, Pinkie brings her friends and Maud to a large obstacle course she constructed, calling it "Pinkie-Rainbow-Rari-Twi-Apple-Flutter-Maud Fun Time." But Pinkie gets stuck and almost gets crushed by a giant boulder. Maud races to save her in a dramatic display, and the other ponies look on in awe. Believing all her efforts to have her friends bond with her sister were fruitless, Pinkie and Maud leave to spend the week at their family's rock farm.

But after witnessing Maud's display, Twilight finally realizes the thing that brings them all together: their love for Pinkie! That's all they really need to be create a bond between them. Everypony agrees, and they surprise Pinkie Pie and Maud by arriving at the rock farm and sharing their realization. They end the vacation by giving Maud rock-candy necklaces for her trip, grateful to have finally have found what they have in common.

Friendship Lesson:

"SOMETIMES, ONE OF YOUR BEST FRIENDS WANTS YOU TO BOND WITH ANOTHER ONE OF THEIR BEST FRIENDS. BUT WHEN YOU MEET THAT FRIEND, YOU REALIZE YOU HAVE NOTHING IN COMMON WITH THAT PONY BESIDES THAT MUTUAL FRIEND....WHEN WE FINALLY REALIZED THAT PINKIE'S HAPPINESS MEANT AS MUCH TO US AS IT DID TO MAUD, THAT WAS ALL WE NEEDED IN COMMON TO BRING US TOGETHER." —TWILIGHT SPARKLE

For Whom the Sweetie Belle Toils

Rarity is hard at work, making dresses for the pop star Sapphire Shores and her backup dancers, and Sweetie Belle is helping out. She knows her big sister is busy, but Sweetie Belle asks Rarity if she has time to please help her finish making the dresses for the Cutie Mark Crusaders' costumes for their upcoming play, which is also Sweetie Belle's debut as a playwright, director, and actress. Rarity looks at the dresses that Sweetie Belle has made and can't help but think that she can improve on them—so when

Sweetie asks for Rarity's help with the finishing touches she's more than happy to!

The play goes off without a hitch, but the Crusaders are a bit peeved that the only thing ponies seem to be talking about are the costumes. Sweetie Belle confronts Rarity and accuses her of trying to steal her spotlight. Rarity is shocked and confused; she thought Sweetie Belle *wanted* her help! Sweetie Belle leaves and tries to sleep but when she can't, she gets up, sneaks into Rarity's room, and ruins the headdress on Sapphire Shores's costume. Sweetie Belle can finally sleep now but has a dream in which Princess Luna shows her the disastrous consequences of her actions. Sweetie Belle wakes up from her nightmare ready to fix her mistake, but Rarity has already left for Canterlot with the dresses!

The Crusaders rush to meet Rarity, and Sweetie Belle gets there just in time to grab the headdress. With a now-waking visit from Luna, she is able to fix it and save Rarity's reputation, to Sapphire Shores's delight. Sweetie Belle apologizes for letting her jealousy get the best of her, and Rarity gladly accepts.

Friendship Lesson:

"I LEARNED THAT JEALOUSY CAN HURT A SISTERLY BOND. I'M JUST LUCKY THAT I HAVE A SISTER WHO'S ALSO MY FRIEND AND THAT FRIENDS FORGIVE EACH OTHER...AND WORK OUT THEIR DIFFERENCES." —SWEETIE BELLE

Leap of Faith

When the Apple family spends the day at the swimming hole, everyone but Granny Smith gets in the water. Despite having once been a very famous swimmer, she is too old and afraid to get in the water anymore. On their way home, they pass the Flim Flam brothers, who claim to have an incredible tonic that is guaranteed to cure anything that ails you. Granny Smith is convinced by their scheme and buys a bottle of the "magical" tonic, much to Applejack and Big McIntosh's chagrin.

Back at the creek, the Apple sisters are shocked to see Granny swimming! Applejack still doesn't trust the tonic and vows to find out what's really in it. Applejack and

Apple Bloom return to Flim and Flam's tent, and Applejack confronts them. They admit their tonic is just apple juice and beet leaves, but also point out that Granny Smith's life has only improved from it. Applejack can't deny that, and she and Apple Bloom leave. Back at the swimming hole, Apple Bloom convinces Granny to enter the Ponyville Swim Meet with her. At the meet, Applejack finds Silver Shill, Flim and Flam's assistant, selling tonic near the stands. He thanks Applejack for teaching him that "sometimes honesty *isn't* the best policy." This wakes up Applejack just as she sees Granny Smith climbing the high dive, preparing to break the Equestrian high-diving record. She manages to stop Granny from seriously hurting herself and tells her the whole truth about Flim and Flam's operation. She tells her and Apple Bloom it was confidence that gave Granny Smith her renewed abilities, not the fake tonic.

Flim and Flam try to convince the crowd that they're not scam artists, but Silver Shill, inspired by Applejack's honesty confesses he was in on it, too. Grateful to Applejack for helping him see the truth, Silver Shill gives her a gold bit with a familiar but mysterious rainbow shine to it.

Friendship Lesson:

"BEING HONEST SURE GETS HARD WHEN IT SEEMS LIKE THE TRUTH MIGHT HURT SOMEPONY YOU CARE ABOUT, BUT I THINK BELIEVING A LIE CAN END UP HURTING EVEN MORE. MAYBE SOME PONIES DON'T CARE ABOUT THAT, BUT I SURE AIN'T ONE OF THEM." —APPLEJACK

Testing, Testing, 1, 2, 3

Rainbow Dash has to study for a Wonderbolts exam she has to pass if she wants to be on the Wonderbolts' reserve team. She hasn't put any time into it and Twilight gets on her case—she *has* to study!

Twilight helps her friend study by doing all *her* usual methods. But flash cards, highlighting, and lectures are not Rainbow Dash's style. It starts to eat away at Rainbow Dash's confidence when she can't seem to remember anything she needs to know for the test. They start bickering, so Fluttershy cuts in and tries to help in *her* way—which involves a play put on by all their pets. This just confuses Rainbow Dash, and eventually, the rest of her friends try to help, but *nothing* works. Not Pinkie Pie's educational rap video, Rarity's fashion show through history...and definitely not Applejack's suggestion to learn about the Wonderbolts through years of experience. All the ponies begin arguing about whose method is best, which drives Rainbow Dash to fly away and leave them all behind.

Twilight joins Rainbow Dash to apologize; she's sorry she overwhelmed her. While flying, seeing Rainbow Dash in her own element, Twilight realizes the best way to get her to learn is in her own environment: in the sky! Rainbow Dash is able to recall facts about the Wonderbolts' history easily when she's flying. Suddenly, everything is clicking and Rainbow Dash is remembering everything she needs to know for the test. She thanks Twilight for all her help, and Twilight tells her Rainbow Dash is the one who did it all on her own. She completes her exam and gets a perfect score, which makes her thrilled and not just a little relieved.

Friendship Lesson:

"THE FACT IS, DIFFERENT PONIES LEARN DIFFERENTLY....ONE WAY OF LEARNING ISN'T BETTER THAN ANOTHER. HAVING A DIFFERENT TECHNIQUE CERTAINLY DOESN'T MAKE YOU DUMB. AFTER ALL, EVERYPONY IS UNIQUE AND INDIVIDUAL!" —TWILIGHT SPARKLE

Trade Ya

The Mane Six go to Rainbow Falls Traders Exchange to trade various items from their own collections: Spike wants to trade a comic book; Rainbow Dash wants to get a first-edition of *Daring Do and the Quest for the Sapphire Statue*; Fluttershy wants to trade a bear call for a bird whistle; Applejack and Rarity want to go in together and combine their items to trade for rare vintage items; and Twilight wants to trade some of her books.

Rainbow Dash finds the book she wants! But she doesn't have enough to trade for it. She and Fluttershy make a lot of different trades all over the venue to try to get the items they really want, but they still come up short. Applejack and Rarity each find a vintage item they want, but they don't have enough, so they start to bicker. Meanwhile, Pinkie Pie has nothing to trade, so she is just focused on making sure Twilight doesn't trade away her books for something not equal in value. Rainbow Dash and Fluttershy get more and more flustered while trying to make the deal for the Daring Do book. Fluttershy drops her bear call in the crowd, and when the Daring Do collector tells them all he wants in exchange for the book is time with Fluttershy, Rainbow Dash agrees! Pinkie continues to promote books with the idea that these books are what made Twilight who she is, which is when Twilight realizes that's exactly why she shouldn't part with them.

Rainbow Dash rushes over and begs Twilight to declare the trade she made for Fluttershy unfair. She has realized nothing is worth the price of a friend! Her plea moves the trader and the deal is undone. Rarity and Applejack give each other gifts that they traded their own goods for. Rainbow Dash reveals to Fluttershy that she ended up getting her the bird whistle. And because the deal fell apart, Twilight gives Rainbow Dash her old paperback copy of *The Quest for the Sapphire Statue*. Rainbow cherishes it even more than the first-edition because Twilight gave it to her.

Friendship Lesson:

"THERE'S NOTHING IN ALL OF EQUESTRIA THAT'S WORTH AS MUCH TO ME AS A FRIEND. I MIGHTA FORGOTTEN THAT FOR A LITTLE BIT, BUT IT'S TRUE....AND MY FRIENDS AREN'T JUST FIRST EDITIONS. THEY'RE ONE OF A KIND." —RAINBOW DASH

Inspiration Manifestation

Rarity's design for Claude, a puppeteer Unicorn, falls short of impressing him, which not only breaks her heart, but also leaves her with no time to make anything for the Foal and Filly Fair. She's been spending every moment making the puppeteer's designs. Spike, ever ready to help his biggest crush, searches for a spell that might help. Spike opens a book he found in a hidden chamber anyway, and finds the "perfect" one. It is called "Inspiration Manifestation," and it "instantly brings ideas to life."

Rarity, desperate, tries the spell. It works right away!

After that, she designs something that pleases Claude and then something great for the Foal and Filly Fair! Spike goes to return the book, but Rarity asks to hold on to it for just a little longer. Rarity goes into full-on manic mode and designs a slew of dresses that overwhelm her boutique. She then turns her attention to Ponyville. She starts with Applejack's cart, then gives Rainbow Dash a dress as she's flying, turns Fluttershy's birdhouse into a mansion, and on from there. Spike is afraid that if he tells Rarity the truth—she's creating more havoc than happiness—she won't want to be his friend anymore.

He sneakily tries to stop her by getting the spell book out from under her without her noticing. But when Rarity catches him, he puts it in his mouth and swallows it. But this still doesn't break the spell! When she crafts four chariots ("Rariots") and plans to spread her designs all over Equestria, he has to tell her the truth: The changes are only making Ponyville worse, not better. She is so shocked by this that the spell wears off. The truth has set them both free, and Rarity tells him he should never be afraid to tell her the truth—they are true friends for life.

Friendship Lesson:

"I LEARNED HOW IMPORTANT IT IS TO BE HONEST WITH YOUR FRIENDS WHEN THEY'RE DOING SOMETHING THAT YOU DON'T THINK IS RIGHT. A TRUE FRIEND KNOWS THAT YOU'RE SPEAKING UP BECAUSE YOU CARE ABOUT THEM." —SPIKE

Equestria Games

The Ponyville team is on their way to the Equestria Games. Spike teaches Apple Bloom, concerned about performing, a trick that makes him feel better when he's nervous—taking a breath and counting to ten. As he's talking to her, he's whisked away by a pair of Crystal Pony royal guards and delivered to Twilight and Cadance at the palace! Because he was so brave saving the Empire from King Sombra, he is now seen as a hero! He will be lighting the torch with his Dragon breath during the opening ceremony. But when the time comes, he gets so nervous, his counting-to-ten trick doesn't help him and he can't light the torch! Twilight, using her magic, does it for him, without Spike knowing, saving him from further embarrassment.

Later, after Twilight tells him what she had to do for him—he thought he had done it with his mind—he is crestfallen. He is feeling more and more useless as the Games go on. He decides to hole up in his bedroom in the Crystal Empire and lick his wounds. Twilight has to retrieve him and drag him out of hiding.

Once out among the crowds, he disguises himself, still ashamed. During the ice archery event, one of the archers accidentally shoots an ice arrow into the sky. The arrow turns a cloud into a large block of ice that careens toward the stadium! No one can stop it! Seeing trouble, Spike forgets himself for a moment and jumps onto the backs of several Pegasi. He shoots the ice with fire, melting it instantly. Everypony cheers, and once again, Spike is a hero. Cadance asks Spike to light the fireworks for the Equestria Games' closing ceremony, and he finally feels pride in what he has done for the Games.

Friendship Lesson:

"NO MATTER HOW MANY TIMES OTHERS TELL YOU THAT YOU'RE GREAT, ALL THE PRAISE IN THE WORLD MEANS NOTHING IF YOU DON'T FEEL IT INSIDE. AND WHEN YOU CARE ABOUT DOING THINGS WELL, YOU CAN BECOME YOUR OWN TOUGHEST CRITIC. SOMETIMES, TO FEEL GOOD ABOUT YOURSELF, YOU'VE GOT TO LET GO OF THE PAST. THAT WAY, WHEN THE TIME COMES TO LET YOUR GREATNESS FLY...YOU'LL BE ABLE TO LIGHT UP THE WHOLE SKY." —SPIKE

Twilight's Kingdom: Part 1

Twilight is feeling bad that her role as princess isn't amounting to much more than waving and showing up at ceremonies. She wants to have a real purpose. Celestia, Luna, and Cadance let her know that her time will come; she just needs to be patient. Back in Canterlot, Rare Find's magic and cutie mark is stolen by Lord Tirek! Luna and Celestia tell Twilight all about Tirek: Originally, he and his brother, Scorpan, came to steal Equestrian cutie marks and magic. Scorpan ended up reforming. Tirek was not reformed, and instead he was sent to prison in Tartarus. Cadance asks Twilight to stop Tirek, but before Twilight can answer, Celestia reveals that she actually has already asked Discord to help.

Hurt, Twilight tells her friends of Celestia's decision. On their way to the Castle of the Two Sisters, they run into Discord. He asks why Twilight has yet to open the Tree of Harmony's chest, saying maybe that has something to do with why she is a princess. Twilight begins searching the old castle library for a means of opening the chest.

Discord appears before Tirek and binds him in chains, surprising him. Tirek tries to convince Discord to join forces, and Discord actually seems to be considering it! Back at the castle, Twilight reads through the friendship journal, and realizes that when each of her friends got a gift, they had to face a situation relating to their Element of Harmony. Twilight realizes their gifts will lead them to the location of the chest's keys! Twilight's friends bring their gifts, and each one becomes a key for one of the chest's keyholes. Unfortunately, there's one key missing: Twilight's. Just then, Spike belches out a letter for Twilight, telling her to go to Canterlot immediately. Twilight meets the other princesses, and Celestia informs Twilight that Discord has joined forces with Tirek. She also tells her that Tirek has gained enough power that he can now steal the magic of all ponies in Ponyville—except Alicorn magic. But once he has the ability to steal that, there will be no stopping him. Celestia has an idea though: The princesses must give up their magic before Tirek is able to steal it from them.

Twilight's Kingdom: Part 2

All the other princesses will give their magic to Twilight so Lord Tirek can't steal it. Tirek doesn't know there is a fourth princess, so he won't come for Twilight at all. Twilight agrees, and the other princesses transfer all their magic to her. Discord and Tirek arrive and discover the princesses have no magic to steal! Tirek banishes them to Tartarus—just as they banished him before. Then, as a sign of true loyalty, he gives Discord a medallion given to him by "someone very close." He sees a stained-glass depiction of Twilight and realizes she is also a princess! Discord tells Tirek where he can find her.

Back in Ponyville, Twilight is not having an easy time managing her new powers. She tells her friends to keep all Ponyville inside while she figures it out. But Discord appears and imprisons everypony. Tirek steals their magic and becomes even more powerful. Discord is thrilled, but Tirek betrays him, locking him up and stealing his magic as well! Discord asks about the medallion, and Tirek says it means nothing to him!

Tirek finds Twilight, and they engage in a fiery battle. Tirek offers her the release of her friends in exchange for her Alicorn magic. It's no question for Twilight, who agrees. Discord, deeply apologetic, gives Twilight the medallion given to him by Tirek. She recognizes what it represents right away! It's the final key! She and her friends race to the chest. The Mane Six turn their keys at the same time and unleash a rainbow-filled vat of magic. With all the new magic, they're finally able to defeat Tirek. Twilight takes on the mantle of the Princess of Friendship and is amazed to find she has a castle of her own.

Friendship Lesson:

"THE MAGIC OF FRIENDSHIP IS ALWAYS WITH ME, AND I HAVE THE POWER TO SPREAD THAT MAGIC ACROSS EQUESTRIA. THAT IS THE ROLE I AM MEANT TO HAVE IN OUR WORLD. IT IS THE ROLE I CHOOSE TO HAVE AS THE PRINCESS OF FRIENDSHIP! WHAT'S WONDERFUL IS THAT I DON'T HAVE TO TAKE ON THAT TASK ALONE. I WILL HAVE MY FRIENDS BY MY SIDE. OUR NEW ROLE IN EQUESTRIA MAY CHANGE A FEW THINGS, BUT IT WON'T CHANGE THE MOST IMPORTANT THING: THE MAGIC OF OUR FRIENDSHIP!"
—PRINCESS TWILIGHT SPARKLE, THE PRINCESS OF FRIENDSHIP

The Cutie Map: Part 1

Princess Twilight Sparkle and her five best pony friends are called to an emergency by the Cutie Map, a magical map in Twilight's castle that lights up whenever there is a friendship emergency. They travel to a village where all the houses except one look exactly the same. The ponies all look the same as well, and each has the same cutie mark—a black equals sign. They are met by two ponies named Party Favor and Double Diamond, who take them to the founder of the village: Starlight Glimmer. Starlight tells the friends that everypony there is unique from anywhere else in Equestria—no pony is special or different from one another. There, equality reigns. She asks if they'd like to join the village and give up their cutie marks, but Twilight and her friends are not interested. As Double Diamond goes to show them the village, Starlight walks away, contemplating how to spread her ominous message of equality.

As the Mane Six take in the village, they discuss how strange it is there, except Fluttershy, who is keeping an open mind. A baker named Sugar Belle notices them "arguing," and they have to explain that they are just having a discussion; it's okay to disagree. They go to Sugar Belle's house and meet with Party Favor and Night Glider, who tell them Starlight Glimmer takes all their cutie marks away with the "Staff of Sameness" and stores them in a vault.

Based on their interest, Starlight Glimmer takes the Mane Six outside the village, to the vault. Once there, they find a large collection of cutie marks stored inside glass casings and a two-pronged staff standing upright. Twilight realizes the Map led them there to save the village and their cutie marks. When Starlight realizes the Mane Six are a threat to her society, she traps them and the villagers surround them. Using the Staff of Sameness, Starlight steals their cutie marks and replaces them with black equals signs. The Mane Six's body colors start to fade and Starlight Glimmer puts their cutie marks in the vault.

The Cutie Map: Part 2

With the loss of their cutie marks, the Mane Six have also lost all their special talents. They decide the best way to escape is to pretend that one of them—Fluttershy—wants to join the village's way of life. Starlight comes to see them, and when Fluttershy asks to be a part of her society, she says she'll let her out—*if* she gives up the names of the ponies who told her about the cutie mark vault. Party Favor takes the blame before Fluttershy can answer, and Starlight locks him up with Fluttershy's friends as punishment.

Later that night, Fluttershy sees Double Diamond bringing the Mane Six's cutie marks in jars to Starlight's house. When Starlight trips over a bucket of water, Fluttershy sees Starlight's equals sign cutie mark is fake! The next morning, Starlight releases Party Favor after he apologizes. Twilight begins to show interest in joining Starlight's society. With this, Fluttershy throws water on Starlight and some of the water splashes on her cutie mark, making it smear. The villagers are furious that she has lied to them the whole time!

Starlight tries to escape with the cutie marks, but with the help of Party Favor, Sugar Belle, Double Diamond, and Night Glider, the Mane Six get them back. The townsponies get their cutie marks back and remember their true selves—now they can befriend one another for who they really are. And just like that, the Mane Six's cutie marks start pulsating, and they can tell that their mission is complete.

Friendship Lesson:

"STUDYING COULD ONLY TAKE ME SO FAR. EACH OF MY FRIENDS TAUGHT ME SOMETHING DIFFERENT ABOUT MYSELF! IT WAS THEIR UNIQUE GIFTS AND PASSIONS AND PERSONALITIES THAT HELPED BRING OUT THE MAGIC INSIDE OF ME! I NEVER WOULD HAVE LEARNED THAT I REPRESENT THE ELEMENT OF MAGIC WITHOUT THESE FIVE!" —TWILIGHT SPARKLE

Castle Sweet Castle

Princess Twilight spends all her time at her friends' houses "helping" them out when she finally admits the truth: She's avoiding her castle. It doesn't feel like home. Rarity suggests their friends redecorate the castle while Spike takes Twilight to a relaxing spa day. Twilight goes off with Spike, and her friends spend the day decorating each room in their own style with the best intentions, oblivious to the mess they are creating. When Spike comes back to see that the decorating has turned the castle upside down, Rarity tells him to keep Twilight away until sundown.

Spike stalls Twilight by taking her on a tour of Ponyville past the ruins of their former home, the Golden Oak Library. Meanwhile at the castle, their friends argue about which decorations to leave and which to give up. They end up just returning the castle back to the way it was in the first place. They realize that they have been decorating it like their own homes instead of how Twilight would like it. This gives Applejack an idea. She and Fluttershy dig up the ground around the library while Rarity, Pinkie, and Rainbow Dash go out and buy decorative gems.

Finally, an annoyed and exhausted Twilight returns to the castle with Spike. At first she can't see any difference in her home, but Applejack tells her what truly makes a home feel like home is the memories you make there! She then reveals that they have made a chandelier out of the Golden Oak Library's roots, decorated it with gems, and hung it in the throne room. Each gem on the chandelier represents a memorable time Twilight had in Ponyville. Twilight is moved by her friend's kindness and finally feels ready to make her castle her home.

Friendship Lesson:

"WHAT REALLY MAKES HOME FEEL LIKE HOME ISN'T WHAT IT LOOKS LIKE. IT'S THE MEMORIES YOU MAKE WHEN YOU'RE THERE." —APPLEJACK

Bloom & Gloom

Apple Bloom informs the other Crusaders that her cousin Babs Seed finally got her cutie mark. The other Crusaders are despondent that they don't have theirs, and Scootaloo puts it in Apple Bloom's head that it's possible she could get one she doesn't even want! At bedtime, Applejack comforts Apple Bloom that any cutie mark she gets will be right for her, and feeling better, Apple Bloom goes happily to sleep.

When Apple Bloom wakes up the next morning, she discovers she finally has her cutie mark! It's a bug-spray can that is used to kill insects called twittermites. This is *not* the cutie mark she wants at *all*! She runs to a dark forest where a voice sounds, asking if she wants it to be taken away. She does! A wind sweeps by, taking it away, and when she returns to Ponyville, she discovers the town has been taken over in a twittermite storm! Apple Bloom wakes up to find out it was all just an awful dream. But this time

she really does have her cutie mark: an apple potion! When she runs to tell her friends she finds out they didn't get theirs and they no longer want to be friends since she's no longer a true Crusader. She goes back to the forest where the voice speaks to her again. Once again she is able to remove her cutie mark, but when she returns she finds her friends now have theirs! They abandon her to go take on their new responsibilities. She finally encounters Princess Luna, who tells her the voice she has been talking to this whole time has been her own shadow.

Taking Princess Luna's advice, Apple Bloom realizes it doesn't matter what her cutie mark will be. Luna shows her that her friends have also been having these fears and the lesson is the same: The cutie mark can't change who they are or their friendships.

Friendship Lesson:

"IF YOU CANNOT ACCEPT WHO YOU ARE, YOUR LIFE MIGHT SEEM LIKE A BAD DREAM." —PRINCESS LUNA

EPISODE 505

Tanks for the Memories

Rainbow Dash is distraught to discover that Tank needs to hibernate for the winter. She can't accept that she's going to lose her pet for an entire season! As all her friends confirm this fact, she gets angrier and angrier. She's determined to find a way to keep him awake. Realizing that he is only hibernating because winter is coming, she decides to just stop winter!

Rainbow Dash does whatever she can: She tries to stop snow clouds from filling the sky; she stops a flock of ducks from flying south for the winter; she stops other Pegasi from making snow; she puts fallen leaves back on the trees; and she tries to keep the weather warm. But none of her efforts work, so she decides to go to winter's source: the Cloudsdale weather factory. But once there, she ends up causing so much damage that the weather all over Cloudsdale becomes completely erratic, and the rest of her friends have to put it back in order.

Rainbow Dash goes home realizing that there's nothing she can do to stop Tank from sleeping for the winter. Her friends try to console her, but Fluttershy tells them that Rainbow Dash just needs to let it out. They give her space to mourn and leave to play in the snow. After a good cry, Rainbow Dash comes to terms with Tank's hibernation, and, before joining her friends in their fun, she reads Tank a bedtime story for his long winter sleep.

Friendship Lesson:

"I LEARNED TO ACCEPT THAT PET TORTOISES HIBERNATE IN THE WINTER! IT HAPPENS." —RAINBOW DASH

Appleloosa's Most Wanted

The town of Appleloosa is excited to set up for their big event of the year: the Appleloosa Rodeo. Applejack is ready to compete and the Cutie Mark Crusaders are considering entering to try to earn their cutie marks. But Sheriff Silverstar is concerned: A tall stack of hay tipped over, nearly injuring all the ponies there, and he believes the outlaw Trouble Shoes might be taking this opportunity to wreak havoc.

This news sends everypony into a tizzy, including Applejack and the CMCs. But the sheriff just amps up his security. The CMCs decide to go look for Trouble Shoes themselves but get lost in the woods. When Applejack can't find them, she recruits the sheriff to look for them, thinking Trouble Shoes might have gotten to them! Meanwhile, the lost ponies are suddenly visited by a large ominous figure. Screaming, they find out it's just a large, very nice Earth pony who turns out to be Trouble Shoes. They realize that Trouble Shoes is no trouble at all and actually just a victim of bad luck. He tells them his cutie mark of an upside-down horseshoe is his curse. The little ponies try to tell him that he's just looking at his cutie mark in a pessimistic way, but before they can convince him, the sheriff comes to arrest him.

The CMCs, determined to help Trouble Shoes realize that his cutie mark is positive, break him out of jail. After Applejack wins the hay-bale stack, the rodeo clowns take the field with Trouble Shoes in tow, and the crowd turns on him. They think he foalnapped the young ponies! The CMCs convince the crowd that Trouble Shoes didn't hurt them, and everypony accepts him for who he is.

Friendship Lesson:

"THE CUTIE MARK CRUSADERS HELPED ME FIND OUT WHAT MY CUTIE MARK TRULY MEANS. TURNS OUT I'M MEANT TO MAKE PONIES LAUGH. SOUNDS GOOD TO ME!" —TROUBLE SHOES

Make New Friends but Keep Discord

The Grand Galloping Gala is taking place in a week, and Discord is distraught to find out that Fluttershy is not taking him as her plus one! She has apparently decided to bring a friend named Tree Hugger instead. He is extremely upset that his best friend clearly doesn't consider him to be *her* best friend. When he gets home, he finds an invitation after all but now has a new problem: He has no one to take! He runs into the only "thing" he can take, the Smooze—which happens to be a large, amorphous gooey liquid of a being—and brings him.

Discord is determined to prove to Fluttershy that he is having the *best* time ever! He pretends desperately that he is not at all jealous or upset, and that he and the Smooze are just the bestest of friends. After a number of shenanigans to make Fluttershy jealous (that don't work), Discord becomes angrier and angrier and more jealous of Tree Hugger and Fluttershy's connection. When the Smooze gets his liquidy substance all over the place and Tree Hugger calms him down to the cheers of all the ponies there, Discord loses his mind. Now *every*pony loves Tree Hugger?

He rips open a portal to another dimension, intending to banish Tree Hugger there, but Fluttershy angrily tells him to stop. Fluttershy tells him that just because she is friends with Tree Hugger doesn't mean she isn't friends with him, too! She helps him see that everyone can have different friends for different occasions. Discord takes this lesson to heart and apologizes to Tree Hugger.

Friendship Lesson:

"THERE'S NO NEED FOR JEALOUSY BETWEEN FRIENDS! EVERYPONY HAS UNIQUE INTERESTS. SOMETIMES A PONY HAS DIFFERENT FRIENDS FOR DIFFERENT THINGS." —FLUTTERSHY

The Lost Treasure of Griffonstone

Pinkie Pie and Rainbow Dash are called by the Cutie Map to the Griffon kingdom of Griffonstone. Rainbow Dash is not very excited about this because Gilda and her friends have not been exactly kind. But when they arrive, they find a run-down town *and* a cranky Gilda and her grandfather, Grampa Gruff. He tells them that Griffonstone used to be a noble city, thanks to the Idol of Boreas. But a monster named Arimaspi stole the idol. The idol was lost when Arimaspi fell into the Abysmal Abyss, and Griffonstone fell into its current state. Rainbow Dash right away assumes that they were sent to Griffonstone to find the Idol of Boreas! She plans a trip into the Abysmal Abyss.

Pinkie finds out from Gilda that the rest of the city doesn't have anything for just fun: no party store, no singing, and no bakery! When Pinkie offers to help her bake, Gilda insists that friendship isn't part of their life there. Pinkie helps her anyway and then goes to find Rainbow Dash. She hears Rainbow Dash yelling in danger and races back to find Gilda for help. Gilda begrudgingly agrees.

Gilda and Pinkie are trying to save Rainbow Dash, when Gilda discovers the Idol of Boreas! She reaches out to grab it, but Pinkie is losing her grasp on Rainbow Dash! Gilda pulls them to safety, and has to sacrifice the idol back to the Abyss. Gilda, realizing the importance of friendship, apologizes to Rainbow Dash and Pinkie for how mean she was. Rainbow Dash accepts, but she is upset that Griffonstone will never be restored without the Idol of Boreas. But Pinkie tells her she is sure that they were sent to Griffonstone not to recover the idol, but to replace it with something better: friendship! With friendship in the kingdom it will be better than it ever has been before.

Friendship Lesson:

"IF YOU CAN LEARN TO CARE ABOUT EACH OTHER AGAIN, GRIFFONSTONE COULD BE A MIGHTIER KINGDOM THAN IT EVER WAS BEFORE" —PINKIE PIE

The 100th Episode!

Slice of Life

Cranky Doodle and Matilda's wedding is happening today but Matilda thought it was tomorrow! Everypony in town is going to the wedding, from Muffins to Dr. Hooves, and now Matilda and Cranky have to race around town to make sure they have all the preparations in place a day early!

Meanwhile, Princess Twilight Sparkle and her friends have to fight a monster that has shown up in town, a bugbear. At the town hall, Bon Bon accidentally reveals her true identity to Lyra Heartstings. It's actually "Special Agent Sweetie Drops," with Bon Bon as her alias, and she has to capture the bugbear that escaped Tartarus. Lyra feels betrayed that her best friend kept a big secret from her, but Bon Bon has to rush off to her covert work. While Cranky and Matilda do the mad dash to get their wedding in order and the rest of the town does as well, Bon Bon manages to capture the bugbear and make it back to the wedding.

The wedding ends up going beautifully with the Mane Six able to attend as well now that the bugbear has been captured. Lyra forgives Sweetie Drops, and Mayor Mare helps the whole town realize that love has brought not only Cranky and Matilda together, but also everypony around them.

Friendship Lesson:

"EVERYPONY IS THE STAR OF THEIR OWN STORY. AND IT'S NOT JUST THE MAIN CHARACTERS IN OUR STORIES THAT MAKE LIFE SO RICH; IT'S *EVERYPONY*—THOSE WHO PLAY BIG PARTS AND THOSE WHO PLAY SMALL." —MAYOR MARE

Princess Spike

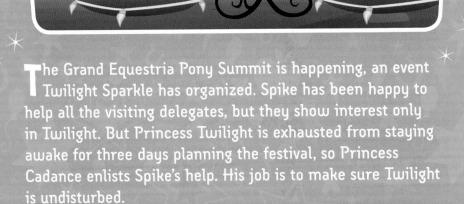

The Grand Equestria Pony Summit is happening, an event Twilight Sparkle has organized. Spike has been happy to help all the visiting delegates, but they show interest only in Twilight. But Princess Twilight is exhausted from staying awake for three days planning the festival, so Princess Cadance enlists Spike's help. His job is to make sure Twilight is undisturbed.

While on duty, Spike stops everypony and everything in Canterlot from making any noise. When two delegates argue, Spike quickly steps in and resolves it. That goes well, but soon more and more ponies are showing up with problems and

Spike is not handling it as seamlessly. Now calling himself Princess Spike, he lets the attention he wanted so badly go to his head and takes advantage of the benefits of the princess lifestyle. He gets massages, has a portrait done of himself, and assumes an attitude of privilege.

When all his decisions go completely awry and an angry mob forms, "Princess" Spike takes responsibility for all he has done and admits the decisions were his alone. The delegates are touched by his speech and after mending a statue that broke under his care, Cadance and a refreshed Twilight see he is contrite and all is forgiven.

Friendship Lesson:

"ONE OF THE MOST IMPORTANT THINGS A PRINCESS CAN DO IS REALIZE WHEN SHE'S MADE A MISTAKE AND FIX IT." —TWILIGHT SPARKLE

Party Pooped

Twilight is very on edge. She is about to visited by royal Yaks from the region of Yakyakistan. They have previously isolated themselves from Equestria, and she really wants to make a good impression on them. But when they arrive, they seem as ill-tempered as ever and destroy the Castle of Friendship's foyer! Twilight enlists Pinkie Pie to make them feel at home until the party she has planned for them later.

Pinkie takes the Yaks around Ponyville, but nothing satisfies them. After many tries to please them with no luck, she decides to go to Yakyakistan and bring some of their home to Ponyville. Maybe that is what is missing from their enjoyment! But she is met with one obstacle after another in getting there, and the entire journey turns out to have been a waste of time. To make matters worse, while she is gone, Spike unwittingly insults the Yaks, making Prince Rutherford declare war on Equestria!

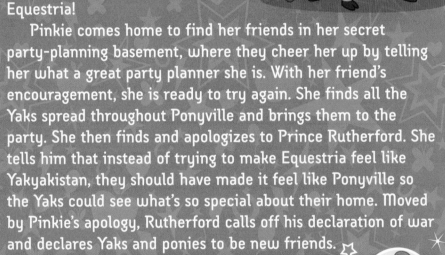

Pinkie comes home to find her friends in her secret party-planning basement, where they cheer her up by telling her what a great party planner she is. With her friend's encouragement, she is ready to try again. She finds all the Yaks spread throughout Ponyville and brings them to the party. She then finds and apologizes to Prince Rutherford. She tells him that instead of trying to make Equestria feel like Yakyakistan, they should have made it feel like Ponyville so the Yaks could see what's so special about their home. Moved by Pinkie's apology, Rutherford calls off his declaration of war and declares Yaks and ponies to be new friends.

Friendship Lesson:

"IT'S IMPORTANT TO MAKE PONIES FEEL AT HOME WHEN THEY VISIT YOU. SHOW THEM WHY YOU LOVE WHERE YOU LIVE SO THEY CAN LOVE IT, TOO! —PINKIE PIE

Amending Fences

When Spike enlightens Twilight to the fact that she wasn't a very good friend to her friends back in her hometown of Canterlot, Twilight decides to go on a trip back there to make amends. When she gets there, she has a wonderful reunion with her old friends Minuette, Lemon Hearts, and Twinkleshine. When Twilight asks where their friend Moondancer is, they all admit they've lost touch with her. Minuette tells Twilight that ever since Moondancer hosted a party and Twilight never showed up, she's become something of a hermit. Twilight feels terrible and vows to make it up to her.

Twilight goes to the Canterlot Library and tries to talk to Moondancer, but she will not give Twilight a chance. It isn't until Twilight performs a spell that makes her take the form of a book illustration that Moondancer agrees to talk to her. Twilight asks if she'll have dinner with their friends. Moondancer says she will go only if Twilight teaches her the spell that turned her into an illustration. Twilight, of course, agrees and she, Moondancer, Minuette, Lemon Hearts, Twinkleshine, and Spike all have dinner that night. Unfortunately, Moondancer's standoffishness doesn't help and the dinner goes horribly. She leaves, stating she shouldn't have bothered giving them a chance; she tried once, but she's now given up on friendship. Twilight knows what she's referring to and feels incredibly guilty once again.

But she also won't give up. Hoping to make up to Moondancer for her big party fail, Twilight recruits Pinkie Pie to create the best party ever. The loving gesture works, and Twilight has a chance to really apologize. This softens Moondancer's heart, and she finally lets all her other friends in again.

Friendship Lesson:

"FRIENDSHIPS ARE ALWAYS WORTH FIGHTING FOR! EVEN ONES THAT MIGHT'VE SOURED IN THE PAST. FIGURE OUT WHAT WENT WRONG AND WORK HARD TO MAKE SURE IT NEVER HAPPENS AGAIN."
—TWILIGHT SPARKLE

Do Princesses Dream of Magic Sheep?

Luna has a nightmare, and in it, she speaks with a small sphere of black smoke called a Tantabus, which eclipses the sun and transforms her back into Nightmare Moon. She wakes up with a start. She quickly learns that the Mane Six all had a dream with the Tantabus that night as well! She explains it is a parasitic creature that exists in nightmares and feeds on and infects dreams. When Luna dreamed of the Mane Six the night before, the Tantabus escaped Luna's dream and invaded theirs! She goes on to explain that the more dreams it feeds on, the stronger it gets. If they don't stop it, it could wreak havoc all over Equestria!

The Mane Six decide to have Princess Luna go into their dreams and pursue the Tantabus into whoever's dream it invades, hopefully catching it and putting it back where it belongs. But Luna can't seem to catch it, and the Tantabus continues to grow. A sobbing Luna admits that she is the one who created the Tantabus in the first place. She did it to punish herself with nightmares after all the trouble she caused when she was Nightmare Moon. Upon hearing that, Twilight and friends let her know that she must forgive herself!

With her friends' love and support, Luna does. This causes the Tantabus to lose its strength and shrink. Luna finally rests, knowing that, even though she isn't perfect, she must be more loving to herself and that she always has the love of her friends.

Friendship Lesson:

"LEARNING TO FORGIVE YOURSELF CAN BE DIFFICULT. DON'T LET YOUR PAST HOLD YOU BACK. LET YOUR FRIENDS HELP REMIND YOU HOW FAR YOU'VE COME AND NEVER STOP GROWING!" —TWILIGHT SPARKLE

Canterlot Boutique

Rarity's dreams are coming true! She is going to open a boutique in Canterlot, where Equestria's most-fashionable ponies live! She has named it the Canterlot Carousel and hired a manager named Sassy Saddles who is putting together the boutique's grand opening. She has a lot of plans for the Carousel's success, including having Rarity do a line of dresses themed after the princesses. Twilight will even model the dress designed after her.

The event goes amazingly well, but Sassy takes over. While Rarity is happy that her Princess Dress went well, she is upset that Sassy took one hundred orders for it. She doesn't love making the same dress over and over; she wants to design new ones. But she also wants to follow her "Rules of Rarity" (putting time, love, and culture into all her projects) and goes through with it. But when one hundred orders turns into two hundred (thanks to Sassy) and nopony wants anything unique added to it, Rarity decides to close the store. This isn't what she got into it for! She has Sassy make going-out-of-business fliers, and Rarity plans her exit.

She has a going-out-of-business sale and puts all her non-Princess Dresses on display. The customers show up and love all her designs! She sees how much her dresses are appreciated and decides not to close the boutique. Sassy sees what she has done to stifle Rarity's creativity and apologizes to her. She goes to leave, as she is sure Rarity doesn't want her running the store anymore, but Rarity takes Sassy's apology to heart. She allows her to stay, as she can see that Sassy finally understands what the "Rules of Rarity" really mean.

Friendship Lesson:

"SOME PONIES LOVE HAVING THE SAME THING AS EVERYPONY ELSE. OTHER PONIES LIKE HAVING SOMETHING UNIQUE! IT'S OKAY TO LIKE BOTH AS LONG AS QUALITY WINS OUT OVER QUANTITY." —RARITY

EPISODE 515

Scare Master

It is Nightmare Night and Fluttershy is all ready for her personal tradition—staying indoors with all the curtains shut. She just has to go out quickly for a couple of items to make sure she has the best night *in* when she runs into her friends. They are so excited to enjoy Nightmare Night together that Fluttershy begins to feel left out and second-guesses her plans for the night. Maybe she can enjoy it if she just gives it a chance!

Her friends are so excited to have her there and plan lots of pregame fun with her in mind. Unfortunately, it's too scary for Fluttershy and she's beginning to doubt her decision to go out with them. When Twilight suggests that Fluttershy be the one to scare *them*, Fluttershy thinks that could be the perfect solution, but her "scare" is just a very awkward tea party. Fluttershy feels this would scare any reasonable pony to death, but the others disagree. The ponies decide that Nightmare Night just isn't for Fluttershy after all, and she agrees to just go have her quiet night at home.

While her friends are off to the big event of the night—the haunted corn maze—Fluttershy secretly takes over it and actually does an amazing job surprising and scaring each and every one of her friends. They are shocked and thrilled to discover Fluttershy was behind it all! But Fluttershy realizes that even though she's good at scaring other ponies, she doesn't enjoy it, and from now on, she will stay safely at home during Nightmare Night.

Friendship Lesson:

"BEING SCARED CAN BE, WELL, SCARY! BUT IT CAN ALSO BE EXCITING. I LEARNED THAT IT'S NO FUN SEEING MY FRIENDS FEEL LIKE THEY'RE IN DANGER, EVEN IF I KNOW THEY'RE NOT. I REALLY DON'T LIKE IT. IT'S JUST NOT MY CUP OF TEA." —FLUTTERSHY

Rarity Investigates!

Rarity and Rainbow Dash are attending a royal dinner at Canterlot castle and Rainbow Dash is so excited to hang out with the Wonderbolts, especially since she's been added as a reserve. At dinner, they meet a retired Wonderbolt named Wind Rider. Rarity notices the scent of his cologne, and Rainbow Dash is star struck. Spitfire comes over and mentions that Rainbow Dash is so talented that she could one day beat Wind Rider's long-distance speed record! At that, Wind Rider leaves the dinner quickly.

The next day Spitfire has been unexpectedly called away by a note sent from her sick mother. Soarin' offers

Rainbow Dash Spitfire's place, and she is beyond excited! This is her dream come true! But it becomes clear that Spitfire was never called away, and her disappearance is mysterious. All  eyes are on Rainbow Dash, and she and Rarity vow to prove her innocence. After an intensive search, Rarity finds many clues: The note from Spitfire's mother had the same cologne scent as Wind Rider! Other pieces of evidence clearly have Wind Rider's mark all over it.

When confronted, Wind Rider confesses. He insists sometimes playing dirty is necessary to preserve your legacy, but none of the Wonderbolts agree, and they are disgusted with his behavior. Rainbow Dash rushes to save Spitfire from missing the show, and when they get back, Wind Rider receives a dishonorable discharge from the Wonderbolts for trying to frame Rainbow Dash. An overjoyed Rainbow Dash takes his place in the show.

Friendship Lesson:

"SOME PONIES THINK YOU'VE GOT TO PLAY DIRTY TO BE THE BEST, BUT THAT'S NOT WHAT BEING A WONDERBOLT IS ALL ABOUT." —RAINBOW DASH

Made in Manehattan

Rarity and Applejack are called by the Cutie Map to Manehattan, much to Applejack's surprise. Why would a country pony like her be called to the big city? When they get there, they find Miss Pommel, who is trying to organize the Midsummer Theater Revival. It is a community-driven play originally created by Bridleway costume designer Charity Kindheart, but she moved away and Miss Pommel has taken over. Miss Pommel now feels as though she's failing because she is overwhelmed and busy with other projects, and she just can't seem to get the community together like Charity could.

Rarity and Applejack offer eagerly to help Miss Pommel. They try to recruit volunteers, but nopony is willing to help.

The costumes haven't been made, and the park where the play is being held is a complete mess. Applejack uses farm skills to fix the park, but even after a whole afternoon of hard work, she barely gets it looking any better. As soon as one of the performers hops on the stage, it collapses.

Miss Pommel feels she's failed to live up to Charity Kindheart's example and loses hope. Applejack tells her and Rarity that they should change tactics: They need to focus on what they *can* do. If they don't have the supplies and the audience, they should downgrade and put on a smaller show. She creates a little stage in the neighborhood square, and the actors put on a play dedicated to Charity Kindheart. It's a huge hit, and everypony remembers the sense of community that Charity was famous for fostering. Rarity points out this is why Applejack was brought to the big city—her country know-how saved the day. Applejack and Rarity's cutie marks start to shimmer, indicating that their friendship mission is complete.

Friendship Lesson:

"THE MANEHATTAN PONIES DIDN'T THINK THEY HAD THE TIME TO DO SOMETHING FOR THEIR COMMUNITY. JUST BY DOING SOMETHING SMALL, YOU CAN MAKE A BIG DIFFERENCE!" —RARITY

Brotherhooves Social

Applejack has been summoned to Manehattan by the Cutie Map, making it impossible for her to compete in the Sisterhooves Social with Apple Bloom. Apple Bloom is devastated, but Big Mac, feeling sorry for himself because Apple Bloom hasn't been as excited about him as she is about their sister, dresses up as "Orchard Blossom" and registers as a mare to compete in the event with her.

Apple Bloom is extremely embarrassed about this development and goes to hide when he registers. But when "Orchard Blossom" actually gets in, Apple Bloom reluctantly participates. As Orchard, Big Mac tries with all his might to win every game the Sisterhooves Social has set up, but "she" can't get them to win at anything. Apple Bloom is getting more and more dejected. She wants to just give up and wait for next year when she can compete with Applejack but "Orchard Blossom" insists that they will win a blue ribbon before the Social is over. The last event is the obstacle course race and so determined to win, "Orchard Blossom" picks up Apple Bloom and plows through every obstacle in their path, literally knocking over ponies in their way. They actually win! But as they celebrate, Big Mac's disguise falls off and they are disqualified.

Back at Sweet Apple Acres, Apple Bloom finds Big Mac sitting alone by a tree, moping. She assures him that she is no longer upset, and she is grateful for what he did for her. He tells her that the only reason he did all this was because he wanted Apple Bloom to look up to him like she used to as a filly, before Applejack became "the hero of the Apple family." Apple Bloom hugs him and tells him he will always be her hero.

Friendship Lesson:

"LET YOUR FAMILY AND FRIENDS KNOW HOW MUCH YOU MEAN TO THEM. THEY'LL SURE APPRECIATE IT!" —APPLE BLOOM

Crusaders of the Lost Mark

The Cutie Mark Crusaders are still obsessed with getting their cutie marks. When Pipsqueak tells them he's running for student president and wants them to be his campaign managers they think this may be their chance to earn them! He finds out that he will be running against Diamond Tiara, who is taking advantage of the fact that her mother, Spoiled Rich, is on the school board. But they clearly are running on different platforms, one for good and one for not so good, and Pipsqueak wins by a landslide.

The CMCs still don't have their cutie marks, but when Diamond Tiara runs off after losing, they are worried about her and follow to make sure she's okay. They find her being berated by her mother for losing. Feeling even worse for her, they invite her to hang out with them. They seem to be a good influence on her, but just then Pipsqueak comes to them, crying that he doesn't have enough money to fulfill his campaign promise to fix the run-down playground. The Cutie Mark Crusaders think Diamond Tiara is going to use this against Pipsqueak, but instead, she races to school, stands up to her mother, and asks her father for the money for the new playground equipment. He agrees, and she announces she is happy to be friends with everypony there.

Apple Bloom realizes that through all their adventures they've always ended up not finding their *own* talents, but helping other ponies find theirs! Just then, the Cutie Mark Crusaders' bodies glow, and in a flash of bright light, their emblem suddenly appears on each of their flanks! They finally have their cutie marks! They are ecstatic, and all Ponyville celebrates with them.

Friendship Lesson:

"HELPING YOUR FRIENDS DISCOVER THEIR TRUE TALENTS CAN BE VERY REWARDING FOR THEM AND FOR YOURSELF! A PONY THAT UNLOCKS THEIR FULL POTENTIAL COULD CHANGE THE WORLD." —APPLE BLOOM

The One Where Pinkie Pie Knows

At Sugarcube Corner, Pinkie Pie finds out that Shining Armor and Princess Cadance are having a baby! But Mrs. Cake tells Pinkie she must keep this news to herself until the couple arrives the next day and shares it themselves. This is obviously very easy for Pinkie Pie! *Not!*

Pinkie Pie is beside herself being around her friends and not allowed to share the news. So she comes up with a solution: avoid them and every other pony at all costs! Mr. Cake reminds Pinkie that she Pinkie Promised to make

cake deliveries around town for him. She does this as best she can without actually seeing anypony and dropping off the deliveries without making any actual contact. She makes it back to the Castle of Friendship and is at breaking point keeping the secret when Shining Armor and Cadance arrive! But they too ask her to keep the secret.

Before Pinkie can get too upset, Shining Armor sends Twilight and her friends on a scavenger hunt with clues that all add up to one thing—the announcement that they are having a baby! Everypony is overjoyed, especially Pinkie, who is thrilled she doesn't have to keep her secret anymore.

Friendship Lesson:

"WATCHING SOMEPONY ELSE BE SURPRISED WITH SOMETHING IS ALMOST BETTER THAN BEING THE ONE WHO'S GETTING THE SURPRISE!" —RAINBOW DASH

Hearthbreakers

Pinkie Pie and Applejack excitedly take the train to the Pie family's rock farm to celebrate Hearth's Warming Eve together with both of their families. They can't wait to share each other's family traditions, and while talking about it, they find out they share the same ones! They both are really looking forward to seeing how their two families mesh.

But when the Apples come over for dinner, they find the Pie family have managed to change all these seemingly universal traditions to be very rock oriented. Applejack talks with her family, and they decide to show the Pies how the Apples do a *real* Hearth's Warming. When the Pies wake up to see all their decorations redone, they are not happy.

Pinkie is stuck in the middle as the families argue. To make matters worse, Applejack had planted her traditional Equestrian flagpole on a fault line, which causes an  earthquake that sends a large, sacred boulder into a quarry. The Apples decide to go home, believing nothing will fix this holiday.

On the train ride back to Ponyville, Granny Smith explains to Applejack just why the Pie family's sacred boulder is so important to them. Applejack realizes she's been discounting how important the rest of their traditions have been to them as well. The Apples all go back to apologize, and the Pies of course accept. They work together to push the boulder to the top of the quarry and celebrate the holidays by combining both of their families' traditions.

Friendship Lesson:

"DON'T PUSH YOUR TRADITIONS ON OTHER PONIES. LEARN ABOUT THEIR CUSTOMS, TELL 'EM ABOUT YOURS, AND THEN MAKE SOME NEW ONES TOGETHER. SHARING TRADITIONS CAN MAKE THE BONDS OF PONYHOOD EVEN STRONGER." —APPLEJACK

What About Discord?

Twilight decides to spend the weekend with Spike relaxing by organizing and reshelving the books in the castle library. She is calling it her "book-sort-cation." Spike doesn't really find that relaxing, but he goes along with it for Twilight. When they emerge from the library, they find that Discord has spent the weekend with the rest of their best friends, forming new bonds plentiful with inside jokes. Spike thinks Twilight is jealous, but she insists she isn't.

The more time she spends with her friends, the more uncomfortable she gets with all the inside jokes and retelling of the great times they had. But she insists that as the Princess of Friendship, she is incapable of jealousy. Twilight decides to take the scientific approach and gathers them all to decipher and break down exactly what it is that is so funny about these inside jokes. When she can't figure it out, she enlists Zecora to give them a potion that will reveal the spell that Discord clearly placed on them. But no spell is revealed, and, in fact, it only brings the other ponies and Discord closer, once again laughing and having a great time. This makes Twilight extremely mad, and she finally admits that she *is* jealous!

Twilight's friends tell her that even though she's the Princess of Friendship, it doesn't mean she's immune to jealousy and that's okay! Discord reveals the truth—he purposefully didn't invite Twilight because he knew that she would learn a lesson about feeling left out that he's had to learn as well. The ponies aren't happy, but they forgive him and all is well with their friendships.

Friendship Lesson:

"IT'S OKAY TO FEEL JEALOUS ABOUT BEING LEFT OUT IF YOUR FRIENDS BECOME CLOSE WITH SOMEONE NEW. THE FIRST STEP IN LETTING GO OF JEALOUSY IS ADMITTING IT! TALK STUFF OVER WITH YOUR FRIENDS, AND YOU'LL WORK IT OUT SOON ENOUGH." —TWILIGHT SPARKLE

The Hooffields and McColts

Fluttershy and Twilight are called by the Cutie Map to the Smokey Mountains, a region of Equestria that is supposed to be very beautiful. They arrive to find most of the trees have been cut down, and there is a longstanding feud going on between the rural Hooffields and the more "city" McColts. They have been firing pumpkins and tomatoes at one another for years, yet no one can really tell why the fight started or who started it. All they care about is winning, and the animals who live in the valley between them are the ones who are suffering the most.

Fluttershy suggests that one side just needs to apologize! The Hooffields pretend to, but it's just a ruse so they can fire a sneak attack. This makes the McColts even madder, and the little animals in the valley continue to get caught in the middle. Fluttershy ends up speaking to the animals and finding out how this fighting began. It turns out the ancestors of the Hooffields and McColts couldn't decide on the best way to preserve and protect the land. They took to opposing mountaintops, and the valley and the animals between them have suffered ever since, due to their constant fighting.

Hearing this story, the present-day Hooffields and McColts wake up to the damage their decades-long dispute has caused to all those around them. They decide to work together to restore the valley and the mountains to their previous glory. And just like that, Twilight and Fluttershy's cutie marks start to glow, indicating the friendship problem is solved!

Friendship Lesson:

"LISTEN TO YOUR FELLOW PONIES, EVEN WHEN YOU DISAGREE ON SOMETHIN'. ALWAYS KEEP AN OPEN MIND. FRIENDSHIP IS SO MUCH BETTER THAN WINNIN' A SILLY ARGUMENT." —MA HOOFFIELD

The Mane Attraction

Applejack is overseeing the Helping Hooves Music Festival, and Pinkie Pie has managed to get Equestria's most famous pop star to perform: Countess Coloratura! Applejack is stunned to realize that this is the same pony she knew as Rara when they were fillies at Friendship Camp. Pinkie mentions Coloratura must have changed a lot since then, because she seems to have turned into quite a diva. Applejack refuses to believe that.

Countess Coloratura arrives flanked by her manager, Svengallop, who won't let anyone, including Applejack, get near her. He comes up with more and more demands for

Pinkie to fulfill on behalf of Coloratura, and creates a show that is more flash than substance. Applejack is finally able to talk to Coloratura and see her true self. She mentions that she can't wait to meet the fillies and colts from the local school who make her whole life possible. But Svengallop becomes even more out of control with his demands, and Applejack can't help but let Coloratura know. At first she refuses to believe it, but Twilight manages to create a spell capturing a particularly vicious diatribe and Coloratura fires Svengallop.

Coloratura has to perform for the first time without a manager and she is beside herself with nerves. But Applejack is there to support her and reassures her that Svengallop was not a true friend. He was only putting out a false image of Coloratura out into the world, and being able to be your true self is what real friendship is about.

Friendship Lesson:

"THE *REAL* PERK OF FRIENDSHIP IS GETTIN' TO SEE YOUR FRIENDS BEIN' TRUE TO THEMSELVES!" —APPLEJACK

The Cutie Re-Mark: Part 1

Princess Twilight is giving a lecture about cutie marks at the School for Gifted Unicorns when she spots Starlight Glimmer in the audience. She and Spike follow Starlight to the throne room where she opens a portal to the past. Twilight and Spike go through it after her and find that she has stopped Rainbow Dash from performing her first Sonic Rainboom, changing time in a way so none of Twilight's friends can get their cutie marks! Before Twilight can confront Starlight Glimmer, Twilight and Spike are sent back to the future.

When they get back, they see how the events Starlight changed in the past made all Twilight's present completely altered. Nothing is the same! In fact Applejack explains that King Sombra declared war against Equestria and the rest of the Mane Six are in Celestia's army! Twilight and Spike go back to the past again, but she can't change anything since Starlight has changed time so whenever Twilight shows up, Starlight will have gotten there first.

When Twilight and Spike return once again to their present day, Ponyville is covered in dense trees in a world run by Queen Chrysalis. They run into Pinkie Pie and Fluttershy, who hold them at bay with spears, accusing them of being Changelings....

The Cutie Re-Mark: Part 2

Twilight and Spike insist that they are not Changelings, but Pinkie and Fluttershy don't believe them—until Zecora intercedes. She is leading the resistance against Queen Chrysalis and proves to Pinkie and Fluttershy that her friends are good. She tells Twilight and Spike go back in time to defeat Starlight.

They return to Cloudsdale in the past, but Twilight once again fails to get Rainbow Dash to create the Sonic Rainboom. They come again, this time to a future where Nightmare Moon rules, and Rarity and Rainbow Dash are her followers. Once again, Twilight and Spike go back to Cloudsdale, but they still can't defeat Starlight. So Twilight tries a new method: She drags Starlight back to Ponyville to have her witness the distorted futures she keeps creating as a result of her actions. But Starlight refuses to believe her. Starlight tells Twilight how she tried friendship once and that pony abandoned her and now she'll never believe in friendship again.

Back in Cloudsdale, Starlight *again* prepares to stop the Sonic Rainboom from happening. Twilight begs her to see she can make new friends and work out problems with them when they arise. The results she saw in those possible futures were proof of how powerful true friendship really is. Twilight tentatively extends her hoof to Starlight, who slowly takes it as she finally lets the Sonic Rainboom occur. Starlight returns to present-day Equestria a changed pony. She agrees to become Twilight Sparkle's first pupil and to learn the magical properties of friendship so she can spread them across all Equestria.

Friendship Lesson:

"THE MAGIC OF FRIENDSHIP CONNECTS ALL OF EQUESTRIA. IF YOU WANT TO MAKE IT AN EVEN BETTER PLACE, GO FORTH AND MAKE MORE FRIENDS!" —TWILIGHT SPARKLE

The Crystalling: Part 1

Starlight Glimmer, now Princess Twilight Sparkle's student of all things friendship, is adjusting to life in Twilight's castle and Ponyville. She asks Twilight what her first lesson is going to be, and after some consideration, Twilight decides upon having Starlight meet up with her old friend, Sunburst, who currently lives in the Crystal Empire. Twilight and her friends are all going there to attend a ceremony called "Crystalling" for Cadance and Shining Armor's baby. It helps strengthen the Crystal Empire's most sacred artifact, the Crystal Heart. It will be a great opportunity for Starlight to heal that friendship. This makes her very nervous, but she agrees to go with them.

The Mane Six and Spike all head out on the train to the Crystal Empire. Twilight takes this time to tell them that the Crystal Heart serves many purposes including protecting the Empire from the frigid cold of the Frozen North. Meanwhile, Starlight is completely beside herself with worry about her upcoming reunion with Sunburst. Twilight is so preoccupied with her duties for the Crystalling that she doesn't listen to Starlight's concerns, and delegates overseeing the reunion to Spike. When Starlight and Sunburst do finally meet, it is awkward and unsuccessful, and Spike can't seem to do anything to make it better.

When they finally arrive at the Crystal Empire's royal palace they discover that Cadance and Shining Armor's foal is an Alicorn! She has intense magical abilities that, as a foal, she can't contain yet. The Mane Six do everything they can to help, but when she gets upset by being separated from Pinkie, her loud cries causes the Crystal Heart to shatter into pieces! As soon as this happens everypony looks out to see ominous snow clouds above that are quickly descending upon the Empire....

The Crystalling: Part 2

The Crystal Heart has been shattered by Cadance and Shining Armor's foal's uncontrollable magic, and now the Frozen North's winter storm has been unleashed. Applejack, Fluttershy, and Rainbow Dash tell all the Crystal Ponies that they must evacuate. Meanwhile, Twilight and the rest of her friends race to the library to find a spell to restore the Crystal Heart.

Back at Sunburst's house, the reunion is still going poorly, with Sunburst bragging and Starlight feeling intimidated. She grabs Spike and leaves, dejected. When they get to the palace, Pinkie tells them what has happened and how threatening the storm is. Twilight and Cadance are no closer to finding a spell to fix the Crystal Heart, so Starlight runs to Sunburst, since he is such an important wizard, to help find a solution. He admits that he actually was a failing student, and he doubts he can help. This gives Starlight the courage to admit her past, and they finally have a healing reunion. This realization gives Sunburst the confidence to go through his spell books, quickly finding a solution!

Sunburst and the gang race back to the castle. He tells everypony that the solution is in the Crystalling ceremony itself! The princesses all cast their magic as the ceremony begins and that, combined with all the love in the room, restores the Heart and dispels the storm. Before they leave to go back to Ponyville, Starlight and Sunburst agree to stay in touch. Twilight feels bad that she wasn't there to help make it happen, but Spike assures her that it worked out perfectly because Twilight gave Starlight the space to make her own decisions—just like Celestia did with her.

Friendship Lesson:

"SOME PONIES LEARN BEST WHEN GIVEN THE SPACE TO MAKE THEIR OWN DECISIONS." —SPIKE

The Gift of Maud Pie

Rarity and Pinkie are going to Manehattan! Rarity is going to find a location for another one of her stores and Pinkie is going to meet Maud. Every time they go to Manehattan together, she and Maud have a "Pie Sisters' Surprise Swap Day" (*PSSSD* for short). Their tradition is to exchange gifts at sunset after having spent a fun day together in the city.

Pinkie knows just what she's going to get Maud: a pouch for one of her rocks! But while Rarity distracts Maud so Pinkie can go to the store, she finds it's closed! She tries to come up with a different gift, but it becomes clear that the pouch really is the best gift of all. Finally, Pinkie sees

a stallion wearing the same pouch that she wanted to get Maud and, after she agrees to trade her party cannon for it, he gives the pouch to her. She's pretty sad about having to give up her most prized possession, but it's worth it for Maud's happiness.

At sunset Pinkie gives Maud the present, and Maud gives Pinkie a carton of cupcake-scented confetti for her party cannon. When she asks Pinkie why she isn't using it, Pinkie eventually admits that she traded the cannon for Maud's gift. They find the pony with whom she traded, and after some angry looks from Maud, he agrees to trade back for the rock pouch. Pinkie Pie is sad that Maud didn't get anything, but *Pinkie* still got a wonderful present! Maud tells Pinkie that all that matters is that she gave her a gift with love.

Friendship Lesson:

"GIFT GIVING ISN'T A COMPETITION. IT'S AN EXPRESSION OF LOVE, AND YOU ALWAYS MAKE SURE TO GIVE GIFTS WITH LOTS OF LOVE." —MAUD PIE

On Your Marks

At the Cutie Marks Crusaders' clubhouse, the friends are at a loss of what to do now that they have their cutie marks. They already know their "special skill," so they don't have to go find it anymore. They decide to go around town and find ponies who need help with *their* cutie marks, since that's what their talent is. But upon searching high and low, they can only find one pony with a cutie mark problem and he is a fast study. Now they're back to square one.

They decide to just have fun until a cutie mark problem arises! They go out on the town, but they're having trouble finding something all three of them want to do. Against

Apple Bloom's wishes, Scootaloo and Sweetie Belle decide to go their separate ways for the day. Apple Bloom is sad at first but then decides to try tap dancing, something she's always thought about doing. She discovers she does love it, but she isn't very good at it. She meets another student there named Tender Taps, who has a lot of talent but an equal amount of stage fright. After talking with the other Crusaders, Apple Bloom realize that maybe Tender Taps is their next assignment!

Apple Bloom goes on stage with him even though she's not a good dancer. Having her with him keeps Tender Taps from being so self-conscious. He gives an impressive performance, and as the crowd cheers, his tap-dancing cutie mark appears!

Apple Bloom feels much better about having separate adventures from her friends, and Sweetie Belle points out that now they'll be three times as likely to find the next recipient of their help.

EPISODE 605

Gauntlet of Fire

Spike hears the "call of the Dragon Lord," which is what the Dragon Lord sounds to beckon all Dragons back to the Dragonlands. Spike isn't thrilled about it considering he knows he'll run into the bully Garble, so Twilight and Rarity go with him, disguised as rocks. When they get there, Dragon Lord Torch, and his daughter, Princess Ember, inform all the Dragons that Torch is stepping down and they are holding a competition called the Gauntlet of Fire. Dragons will complete for the title of Dragon Lord. Princess Ember would love to just take over and not hold any such competition, but her father has forbidden it.

Spike is ready to leave since he has no interest in being

the Dragon Lord, but when he hears Garble and other Dragons talking about nefarious plans, he realizes he must stay and compete to ensure the safety of Equestria's ponies. In the first leg of the competition, Spike saves a disguised Princess Ember from drowning. She is not happy about having an ally or that Spike has pony friends with him, saying, "Dragons don't do friends." Still, when Garble happens upon the group and almost discovers Rarity and Twilight, she covers for them. Spike and Ember pair up until the last leg, when she is so upset by his friendship with ponies that they part ways. Spike is devastated; he thought they really were friends! He is at the end of the competition—the center of a volcano—when Garble, right behind him, takes over and is about to drop Spike into it. Just then, Ember saves Spike and sacrifices her own win. She has Spike go ahead and take the prize.

Ember finally understands what friendship really is and Spike, not ever wanting to be Dragon Lord in the first place, passes the role on to Ember. He knows she will be a great leader and keep Equestria safe. Ember lets him know that he will always have a friend in the Dragonlands.

Friendship Lesson:

"IT TAKES MORE THAN JUST BEING BIG AND STRONG TO BE A GOOD DRAGON LORD!" —PRINCESS EMBER

No Second Prances

Starlight Glimmer has been assigned by Twilight Sparkle to make new friends in Ponyville: the very first task Princess Celestia assigned Twilight! Twilight is having a dinner party that night for Celestia, and Starlight is to bring a new friend to dinner to show her how she's progressing in her friendship lessons. So she sets off through Ponyville to make a new friend. She tries as hard as she can but is failing until she runs into a pony with a dark past who is finally a pony with whom Starlight feels at home. Twilight is not so happy to find out this friend is none other than...the Great and Powerful Trixie.

Although Trixie explains she is on an "apology tour," Twilight is nervous about Starlight's new friend being someone with a bad reputation. Starlight tells Twilight she should trust her like Celestia trusted Twilight! She goes off to spend more time with Trixie, whose apology tour is also a magic tour. She has a show coming up about which she is nervous, and Starlight offers to be Trixie's assistant to make her feel more comfortable. The only problem is, it falls on the same night as the dinner party to which she's supposed to bring Trixie, and when she doesn't show up for it, Twilight comes looking for her. When Twilight confronts Trixie, Trixie says she has only good intentions, but then admits that maybe a part of her became friends with Starlight just to beat Twilight at something. Starlight runs away, crying, and Twilight is upset for being partly responsible for driving apart Trixie and Starlight.

Twilight runs to find Starlight and apologizes. She should have trusted her more, and she does think Trixie meant well. They go back to find Trixie, who also apologizes and calls Starlight her best friend. They hug, and this gives Twilight a chance for *her* apology to Trixie for not trusting her.

Friendship Lesson:

"GIVE PONIES THE FREEDOM TO MAKE THEIR OWN DECISIONS, AND THEIR OWN FRIENDS. DON'T TRY TO PICK AND CHOOSE THEIR FRIENDS FOR THEM." —TWILIGHT SPARKLE

Newbie Dash

Spitfire offers Rainbow Dash a full-time position on the Wonderbolts and she is thrilled! Fire Streak has retired and now it's Rainbow Dash's shot! But during the first practice for an upcoming event, she goes into show-off mode and crashes into a garbage can. Humiliatingly, this gets her back her old nickname from flight school: Rainbow Crash.

When she gets home, her friends see how sad she is and Twilight tells her she should stop putting the Wonderbolts on a pedestal and just treat them like her friends. Rainbow Dash tries that approach, but she takes it too far, making fun of them and doing impressions of them that they don't appreciate. She's feeling worse and worse, and by the time the show comes, she is desperate to show them she deserves her place on the team. She enlists Scootaloo in her plan to throw up a storm cloud during the big event so she can put on a lightning display and really stand out. But that, too, backfires and she ends up crashing once again.

While Spitfire is not happy that Rainbow Dash changed the routine for the big show without asking, all the Wonderbolts assure her that she needn't have gone out of her way to prove herself! She has already proven herself by being an amazing flier and saving Equestria numerous times! They also tell her that having an embarrassing nickname is just part of fitting in. They all have one! Rainbow Dash realizes trying so hard to stand out isn't necessary when you're part of a team. She can finally truly enjoy being a Wonderbolt.

Friendship Lesson:

"I SPENT MY WHOLE LIFE TRYING TO BE A STANDOUT FLIER, BUT NOW THAT I'M A WONDERBOLT, IT'S TIME TO BE OKAY WITH FITTING IN!" —RAINBOW DASH

A Hearth's Warming Tail ♥ ♥ ♥

☆ It's Hearth's Warming Eve in Ponyville and everypony is excited about it—except Starlight Glimmer. She doesn't see the point in it other than it being a silly excuse to sing songs and have "fun." To get her friend into the spirit, Twilight Sparkle reads her favorite holiday story, *A Hearth's Warming Tale*.

As she reads, Starlight is transported into the story, where her friends reenact the tales in her imagination. She learns about Snowfall Frost (Starlight Glimmer), who also does not get the point of the holiday and gathers materials for a magic spell, to get rid of it forever! Just before she casts the spell she is visited by the Spirit of Hearth's Warming Past (Applejack), who tells her that every choice we make has consequences. She shows the past where Snowfall was happy and excited to celebrate! But when her magic teacher, Professor Flintheart, found her celebrating, he told her no serious student of magic would waste their time on a frivolous holiday. She then meets the Spirit of Hearth's Warming Presents (Pinkie Pie), who teaches her about thoughtfulness and learning to love the present moment. Then she is visited by the Spirit of Hearth's Warming Yet to Come (Luna), who shows her that in a world where she cast her spell, she now has no friends and her spell has unleashed the Windigos. Snowfall asks to see another future, but there is none. When she gets home, she realizes the future is hers to create and how important celebrating happily with friends really is.

Realizing now that she must let go of her past thoughts about the holiday and enjoy the present moment with her new friends, Starlight Glimmer joins everypony in celebration. Everypony is happy to see her and ready to enjoy Hearth's Warming Eve together!

Friendship Lesson:

"[HEARTH'S WARMING EVE ISN'T] ALL ABOUT SINGING AND PRESENTS. THE SINGING AND PRESENTS ARE ALL ABOUT CELEBRATING THE PONIES IN OUR LIVES. THE PONIES WE SHOULD LISTEN TO MORE OFTEN: OUR FRIENDS." —STARLIGHT GLIMMER

EPISODE 609

The Saddle Row Review

It's the day after Rarity's new store, Rarity For You, has had its grand opening in Manehattan, and the newspaper has published a tell-all of what led up to it. The rest of the Mane Six run to stop Rarity from reading it. They were all involved in the debacle leading up to it and have managed to keep her from finding out all the grisly details. When they get to Rarity's house, they find she has the paper but even though she hasn't read it, she insists on doing so then. As she reads, the group sees the events that transpired the day before.

As they go one day in the past, Rarity prepares for her

big day. Before she can even begin, a slew of problems arise. From a family of raccoons making their home in one of her boutique's back rooms, to DJ Pon-3's noisy dance club being above the store, to her clothes arriving in a disorganized mess, nothing is going right. Twilight suggests postponing the grand opening, but Rarity insists on keeping the date the same. At one point Twilight has to lock Rarity in the window display so she can't freak out and see the mess that is taking place hours before her grand opening. The rest of the group does everything in their power to fix all the issues, but it only gets worse. It's only when Twilight realizes they've been trying to solve everything how they think Rarity would want them to and not in their own ways, that they finally find the solutions to all the problems.

Twilight lets Rarity out of the window display room so she can see what a beautiful job her friends have done. Relieved and thrilled to see the boutique looking like perfection, she opens Rarity For You to the public. Back in present day, she stops reading the review and tells her friends she's not mad at all; in fact, she's beaming with pride! Her store wouldn't be what it is without her friends' contribution.

Friendship Lesson:

"DON'T BE AFRAID TO TRUST A PONY TO SOLVE A PROBLEM THEIR WAY." —TWILIGHT SPARKLE

Applejack's Day Off

Applejack would love to join Rarity at the La Ti Da Spa for a spa day in the steam room, but once again she is stuck at the farm with a leg's length of chores to do. Twilight and Spike offer to help out on the farm so she can have a relaxing day with Rarity and take a break for once! Applejack isn't sure but finally agrees and gives them pages of detailed instructions before she leaves with Rarity.

When they get to the spa, there is a long wait as the steam room is working at half strength. The customers are all standing outside of the room, freezing as they wait their turn. Aloe, the manager at the spa, hands out hot towels to help them warm up. Applejack does some investigating and figures out quickly that the problem in the steam room is because of a leaky pipe. This is causing the need for hot towels, which is using up the hot water normally

used for steam, which means the washing machines are also needed, using even more hot water! She fixes the problem and Aloe is relieved, realizing they had gotten so used to the way things were, they couldn't see there was even a problem. Unfortunately, there's no time left and their spa day is once again wasted.

Ironically, when Applejack gets back to the farm, she finds Twilight and Spike having a difficult time with her instructions on how to feed the pigs. She in turn realizes that, like Aloe, she, too, has made it more difficult than it needs to be! She hadn't realized how many problems were being unnecessarily created that she was just living with. With everyone free of their duties, Applejack is finally able to have a real spa day with Rarity!

Friendship Lesson:

"I GUESS I JUST GOT SO USED TO DOIN' EVERYTHIN' A CERTAIN WAY, I DIDN'T REALIZE THERE WERE ANY PROBLEMS." —APPLEJACK

Flutter Brutter

Fluttershy is very upset that her brother, Zephyr Breeze, is moving back in with their parents just as they are enjoying their retirement. He is clearly not trying very hard to get a job, and is putting a large burden on them. After Fluttershy gives him a talking-to, she is shocked when he shows up on her front door, taking their conversation to mean that he should move in with her!

She allows him to stay if he gets a job. He agrees, and Fluttershy sets him up at the Carousel Boutique "helping out" Rarity. Zephyr makes a mess of the place, and Fluttershy is humiliated. She then tries Twilight, but he dumps all the work on Spike so he can do his own thing. Finally, she brings him to

Rainbow Dash, who threatens to zap him with lightening if he fails at his task. When he returns to Fluttershy's cottage with a zapped mane, Fluttershy makes him leave.

He retreats to the Everfree Forest, where Fluttershy takes pity on him. He confesses the truth: He's just been so afraid to try because he could never live up to his sister's success as a hero in Equestria. Fluttershy tells him that she knows he can be a success. And that sometimes you have to try even if it means you end up failing. He takes their talk to heart and appreciates all Fluttershy has done to help him.

Friendship Lesson:

"SOMETIMES YOU HAVE TO DO THINGS, EVEN THOUGH YOU MIGHT FAIL." —FLUTTERSHY

Spice Up Your Life

Pinkie Pie and Rarity are called to Canterlot to solve a friendship problem! When they get there, they follow Pinkie Pie's stomach growls to Restaurant Row. There, they find restaurant after restaurant with all the same foods and décor, and also with the same three-hoof rating. Apparently, food critic Zesty Gourmand has been using her influence on making or breaking restaurants to make every restaurant the same, even though they have the same mediocre flavors. They finally find a father/daughter-run restaurant called the Tasty Treat without any rating that Pinkie finds delicious. But they quickly discover the father, Coriander Cumin, and the daughter, Saffron Masala, have been fighting because of the lack of business. Rarity and Pinkie think they have found their friendship problem!

Rarity offers to bring Zesty to the restaurant to judge their food and give them a rating, but she will only come that very night. They scramble to get everything in order. Rarity stays behind with Saffron and convinces her to conform to the other restaurants to get a good review, and Pinkie goes out with Cumin to rustle up some customers and encourages him to break the trend and create unique food. When they all reconvene, they find themselves at odds once again. Then Zesty shows up, is subject to the group's angry meltdowns, and leaves in a huff.

Having failed in their efforts, they all apologize to one another. Saffron makes Coriander a family recipe to cheer him up, and they bond over the reason they wanted to open the restaurant in the first place. Rarity realizes her mistake and encourages them to have a grand re-opening exactly in the style of food that they love. It's a huge hit, and the other chef ponies on the Row, seeing how happy Saffron and Corriander are being true to themselves, are inspired to cook in their unique styles as well. Pinkie and Rarity's cutie marks glow, and they know their mission has been a success!

Friendship Lesson:

"JUST BECAUSE YOU LIKE YOUR FOOD A CERTAIN WAY, THERE IS NO REASON TO TELL OTHER PONIES THAT THEY NEED TO DO THE SAME!" —RARITY

Stranger Than Fan Fiction

The Daring Do Convention is happening, and Rainbow Dash is beside herself with excitement! She meets a pony named Quibble Pants, who bonds with her over their love of Daring Do. However, she quickly finds out that he only loves the original trilogy, claiming that everything after that is unrealistic. Rainbow Dash tries to defend her hero, but can't without revealing that A. K. Yearling is actually Daring Do! The two can't agree and decide they really weren't meant to be friends after all.

Rainbow Dash finds A. K. Yearling to help convince Quibble how good the other books are, but A. K. is embroiled in another adventure. She has found a key and is certain it will unlock a treasure; she just has to get to it before the evil Dr. Cabelleron does. She asks Rainbow Dash to look out for any suspicious characters while at the convention. While on that mission, Rainbow Dash runs into Quibble again. Dr. Cabelleron overhears them talking about the key and foalnaps them! When Quibble almost dies in a raging rapid, he begins to realize this is definitely not fiction. When Daring Do appears at another treacherous moment and saves them, Quibble is relieved that the adventure can end. But Daring Do tells him she needs to finds her treasure! Thanks to everypony working together, she gets what she came for and they finally can go back home.

Quibble now can't help but admit that the later books are more realistic than he realized. He still doesn't *like* them, but he can respect them. Through all the adventure he experienced, he realized it's okay for Rainbow Dash and him to like the series in their own way, and that shouldn't keep them from being great friends.

Friendship Lesson:

"WE DON'T HAVE TO AGREE ON EVERYTHING TO GET ALONG." —QUIBBLE PANTS

The Cart Before the Ponies

t the Schoolhouse, Miss Cheerilee informs all the ponies
that the Applewood Derby is coming up! All the colts and
ies will build their own carts and race on a racetrack
th an older pony helping them out. Sweetie Belle, Apple
om, and Scootaloo immediately enlist the help of Rarity,
lejack, and Rainbow Dash and prepare for the big race!
Almost immediately, the older ponies start instituting
r own ideas of what they want into the carts. Though the

fillies don't like it, they don't feel confident enough in their own ideas to challenge the older ponies. The older ponies get more and more aggressive about their own choices and end up designing the carts without any input. The Crusaders feel even more dejected when the race begins and Rarity, Applejack, and Rainbow Dash literally take the wheels with the fillies in the backseats! The Crusaders are not having fun, and blinded by intense competition, the older ponies get out of control and crash their carts!

The younger ponies finally admit their true feelings. They tell their mentors they knew they should have spoken up sooner, but they assumed the older ponies knew best, having participated in the Derby before. Applejack, Rainbow Dash, and Rarity feel terrible and apologize. They also convince Cheerilee to agree to a second Applewood Derby to make up for the first one, and this time, the Crusaders ride their own carts with everypony cheering on the sidelines.

Friendship Lesson:

"YOU MUSTN'T THINK OLDER PONIES AUTOMATICALLY KNOW BEST. IT'S OK TO SPEAK UP FOR YOURSELF." —RARITY

28 Pranks Later

Rainbow Dash is pranking everypony, and the only one who doesn't seem to mind is Pinkie Pie. Twilight and friends gather to tell Rainbow Dash that a prank is not funny if the pony involved doesn't think so. Rainbow Dash is not getting the point and in fact pranks Twilight during the discussion! Rarity tells her that if she can't pull off a prank everypony enjoys then she shouldn't do it at all. Much to Rarity's chagrin, Rainbow Dash takes that as a challenge.

Rainbow Dash goes prank nuts and pulls off pranks on practically everypony in town. Pinkie Pie has to tell Rainbow Dash to stop this pranking nonsense. She heads to Rainbow Dash's house but before Pinkie can confront her,

Rainbow Dash tells her about her next prank. She is going to replace all the cookies being sold during the Filly Guide Cookie Drive with cookies that give everypony who eats them "rainbow mouth," making their mouths and teeth turn rainbow colors. Pinkie tries to convince her not to go through with it. Of course Rainbow Dash doesn't listen.

After pulling the prank, Ponyville gets strangely quiet. Rainbow Dash ventures out to find the entire town has gotten sick from the cookies! She finds a vast amount of ponies desparate for cookies! Rainbow Dash tries to let them know it was just a prank and she didn't intend for this to happen, but even her best friends are now zombified! Suddenly, the ponies drop their act and Pinkie reveals it was a prank she came up with, and everypony but Rainbow Dash was in on it. Because Rainbow Dash doesn't see the humor in this prank, she realizes how she has been making everypony feel with her own pranks. She knows now that nopony should get a laugh at another pony's expense.

Friendship Lesson:

"I LEARNED THAT YOU CAN'T JUST GO AROUND PRANKING WHOEVER YOU FEEL LIKE WITHOUT THINKING ABOUT HOW IT MIGHT MAKE THEM FEEL. PRANKS CAN BE A LOT OF FUN BUT ONLY WHEN EVERYPONY HAS A GOOD TIME." —RAINBOW DASH

The Times They Are a Changeling

Twilight Sparkle, Starlight Glimmer, and Spike all go to the Crystal Palace to see Flurry Heart, Twilight's new niece. But when they get there they find the whole town in a tizzy. A Changeling has been spotted! Since they feed on love and there is now more love in the Crystal Empire than ever since the Crystalling ceremony, the citizens are terrified of what will happen. Spike, a hero to Crystal ponies everywhere for finding the Crystal Heart, goes to find the Changeling.

   After a long search Spike does find him! But it turns out

that this Changeling is actually...nice? His name is Thorax and after coming there during the Crystalling incident he fell in love with the Crystal Empire, and has truly never felt like a Changeling his whole life. Spike is excited to show all the Crystal ponies that they have nothing to fear, but nopony believes him! You obviously can't trust a Changeling! Spike is afraid to risk his reputation as a hero so he doesn't put his foot down. Instead he tries to do it sneakily: He has Thorax "change" into a nice pony and convince everypony that way. This backfires, and when Thorax is around the intense love of Flurry Heart he can't help but lose his disguise. All the ponies turn on him and he flees.

Spike finds him back in his cave, and Thorax comes out hissing; he never should have trusted Spike. Spike feels terrible for not having stood up for Thorax as he is and runs back to the Crystal Empire to defend him. Singing a song that expresses Changelings are as capable of change and good as any other creature, he convinces everypony of Thorax's goodness. Twilight is proud of Spike for risking his celebrity reputation for his new friend, and the royal family accepts Thorax as a citizen of the Crystal Empire.

Friendship Lesson:

"A NEW FRIEND CAN COME FROM ANYWHERE." —SPIKE

Dungeons & Discords

Discord shows up to have tea with Fluttershy but finds her packing her bags for a trip to Yakyakistan. She's been called away at the last minute for a friendship tour there. Discord doesn't know what to do with himself while she's gone, so she suggests joining Spike and Big Mac for the guys' night they have every once in a while. Discord doesn't like the idea of hanging out with the "uncool sidekicks" but changes his mind when he sees them at the train station and they convince him it might actually be fun.

When he gets there all dressed up and ready to go, he is very disappointed to find out they are intending to just stay in and play Ogres and Oubliettes, a role-playing game. It *is* going to be nerd central after all. Spike explains that the game is one where they create their own fantasy personalities and go on imaginary adventures. Discord can't think of anything duller until the idea occurs to him—make it real! He transports Spike and Big Mac into the game itself. Discord is in control of the whole game, and all the danger is now real. They hate this and yell at Discord for ruining their game. They only asked him there because they felt sorry for him in the first place, and now he's trying to take over!

Discord feels terrible with the realization that *he* is actually the not-cool one! He was a pity invite! Spike and Big Mac feel bad that he's taking it so hard. They admit it actually was fun when the game was real, but could he just not make it as scary? He excitedly agrees and when the Mane Six come back they find the three guys in a raucous game of toned down, real-life Ogres and Oubliettes.

Friendship Lesson:

"IT NEVER HURTS TO MAKE NEW FRIENDS." —FLUTTERSHY

EPISODE 618

Buckball Season

Applejack has been taunted by her cousin Braeburn that his team in Appleloosa could defeat Ponyville's team at the sport of buckball. She and Rainbow Dash have taken great offense to this and decide to start practicing to beat them in the Ponyville—Appleloosa Showdown. But while doing so they discover that the best team really would consist of Fluttershy, Pinkie Pie, and Snails. Applejack and Rainbow Dash don't care who's on the team as long as they win, so they decide to make Fluttershy, Pinkie Pie, and Snails the Ponyville team, and Applejack and Rainbow Dash will coach them.

But during the practice they put so much pressure on Fluttershy and Pinkie Pie to win that they start losing their touch. They drop balls they never would have before and shut down in general. Only Snails is immune to the heat he's getting from the competitive coaches. On their way home, Pinkie and Fluttershy confide in each other how worried they are about letting down their friends. They take some relief in the fact that hardly any ponies have even heard of the sport until they get to the train station and see a crowd of ponies cheering for them as they set off for Appleloosa. Seeing how upset Fluttershy and Pinkie Pie are, Applejack and Rainbow finally realize that they've taken out the all the fun of the game and tell their friends they'll trade places with them to compete.

Fluttershy and Pinkie Pie eagerly agree and also agree to help them out by practicing with them before the game. With the pressure off, they're back to their great-buckball-playing selves and realize they play well when they don't think about trying to play well. Applejack and Rainbow Dash tell them that's what they were trying to prove by having them think they weren't going to compete! They still can if they want to. With that insight, Fluttershy, Pinkie Pie, and Snails agree to compete again, and they win the game against the Appleloosa team.

Friendship Lesson:

"SOME PONIES THRIVE ON PRESSURE AND SOME PONIES DON'T. AND HAVING FUN IS WHAT MAKES YOU REALLY, REALLY, REALLY GOOD!" —RAINBOW DASH

The Fault in Our Cutie Marks

The Cutie Mark Crusaders are certain there is no cutie mark problem they can't solve—until they meet a mail-carrier Griffon named Gabby. She is desperate to get her cutie mark and heard the Crusaders were who she should turn to in order to make her dream come true. After consulting with Twilight, the Crusaders' suspicions are confirmed—no non-pony can get a cutie mark. They reluctantly tell Gabby this, but her optimism is undeterred. She just *knows* if she tries hard enough she'll get that cutie mark. The Crusaders, buoyed by her enthusiasm, agree to try to help her.

They discover Gabby has what should be a good problem—she's great at everything! The Crusaders tell her that this makes it nearly impossible to single out her one special talent. They finally have to tell her that what they said before was true. She will never get her cutie mark. She leaves in tears, but comes back soon after to reveal that she suddenly got her cutie mark! After celebrating, they quickly realize it's a fake. She tells them she only did it because she felt awful that they felt so bad about not being able to help her.

With that, Scootaloo quickly realizes that Gabby *does* have a special talent! It's helping others in need, just like the Crusaders' special talent! What makes a special talent is something you love doing, and she doesn't need a cutie mark to prove that. With that realization, the Crusaders give her a a hoofmade gift: the design of the CMCs' cutie marks carved into clips for her mailbag. It's a makeshift cutie mark, but it means the world to her. Gabby, now a full-fledged member of the Cutie Mark Crusaders, promises to come back soon to help them out!

Friendship Lesson:

"FINDING YOUR SPECIAL PURPOSE DOESN'T HAVE TO BE ABOUT *BEING* GOOD AT SOMETHING. IT'S ABOUT *FEELING* GOOD ABOUT SOMETHING INSIDE." —SCOOTALOO

EPISODE 620

Viva Las Pegasus

pplejack and Fluttershy are not pleased to learn they have
been called by the Cutie Map to the party city of Las
gasus. It's noisy and crowded and not their idea of a good
ne. Once there, they go to the party resort in the center of
city and quickly meet Gladmane, its owner. They don't
d him to be very genuine, but they allow him to take them
und so they can find their friendship problem and get out
here as quickly as possible.

They discover that Flim and Flam are there and are no

longer on speaking terms. Gladmane tells them this has been the case since they arrived at the resort. Fluttershy believes this is the friendship problem they were called for, but Applejack has *no* interest in helping them. She believes they're better apart than together and leaves to find other ponies to help. Fluttershy and Applejack soon find that there are *many* ponies there with seemingly irreparable friendship problems. It seems that Gladmane benefits from these problems because as long as the ponies stay angry with one another, they are forced to stay at his resort and make him money. He is managing to keep them at odds behind their backs so they never discover he is the one behind their disagreements. After a few tries, Applejack and Fluttershy successfully manage to expose his lies and reveal his true nature to everypony in the resort.

Once they're aware of who is behind their disagreements all the ponies resolve their issues with one another and quit Gladmane's establishment. Applejack and Fluttershy's cutie marks start to glow, meaning they have solved the friendship problems!

Friendship Lesson:

"DON'T GO EXPLOITING PONIES' DISAGREEMENTS TO MAKE YOURSELF LOOK BETTER. YOU MIGHT JUST LOSE YOUR BUSINESS AND REPUTATION OVER IT." —APPLEJACK

Every Little Thing She Does

Princess Twilight is teaching Starlight magic lessons and points out that it's been a while since she's tackled her friendship lessons. Twilight tells her today is the perfect day to get back to it as she has to go to Canterlot, so Starlight can work on it while she's gone. Starlight tells her that won't be a problem—it's a cinch! And after Twilight and Spike leave, she plans to tackle not one but *five* friendship lessons.

She invites Rarity, Fluttershy, Applejack, Pinkie Pie, and Rainbow Dash to the castle to help her with sewing, animal care, scrapbooking, baking, and chillaxing, respectively. Applejack thinks Starlight is taking on more than she should handle at once, but Starlight insists she can do it. She then attempts to perform a task with each of them, but the ponies each have their own ideas for how they want to do things, and Starlight can't handle it. She casts a spell to have them under her influence so they'll easily comply with her instructions. But things get out of control when each pony makes a mess, and Twilight returns to see her entire castle in disarray. Starlight can't figure out what went wrong! She must have cast the spell wrong....Twilight says she missed the entire point. She was supposed to be spending time with each pony and getting to know them, not performing tasks. Starlight finally understands and feels awful about letting down everypony.

She goes to apologize to everypony for using her magic to control them. She is still so new to this whole friendship thing. They can see how sorry she is and offer to help her clean up. While doing so they all bond for real, and without knowing it, Starlight has just succeeded at her friendship lesson!

Friendship Lesson:

"DON'T CAST SPELLS ON YOUR FRIENDS!" —RAINBOW DASH

P.P.O.V. (Pony Point of View)

Twilight is excited to meet Applejack, Rarity, and Pinkie Pie at the train station when they get back from their boat trip to Seaward Shoals! She can't wait to hear what affect "getting out of their element" had on them. But when they arrive, the three ponies angrily trot off in different directions.

Twilight and Spike go to Rarity's to hear what happened. In her retelling, she took her friends on the boat trip as a surprise. But according to her, after Rarity offered her friends cucumber sandwiches, Applejack tossed them overboard, laughing. In her description, after that, everything that went wrong was Applejack's fault and resulted in the ship capsizing. Twilight is suspicious of this retelling and goes to Pinkie Pie. The only things similar in Pinkie Pie's version of the story are the cucumber sandwiches and the ponies going overboard. But according to Pinkie, *she* was the one who took them to get out of their element, and everything that went wrong was *Rarity's* fault. Twilight doesn't believe this, either, and goes to Applejack to get her account. Once again, the only things similar in the story are the cucumber sandwiches and the ponies going overboard.

Twilight manages to get the ponies in the same place and tells them she knows what happened. First of all, the reason their ship went overboard was because cucumber sandwiches are the favorite food of the tri-horned bunyip that lives in those waters! And when it surfaced to eat the food, it caused a tidal wave! When the ponies say this doesn't explain their disagreements, Twilight says each pony was trying so hard to bring the other two out of their element that they didn't notice the others doing the same. The three ponies realize how much they've overlooked their friends' efforts and make up.

Friendship Lesson:

"EVEN LONGTIME FRIENDS NEED TO WORK ON COMMUNICATION!" —TWILIGHT SPARKLE

Where the Apple Lies

When Apple Bloom tells a "white lie" Applejack reassures her that while she shouldn't have done it, Applejack herself told a very tall tale when she was a filly. Apple Bloom doesn't believe it, but Big Mac and Granny Smith back her up and tell the story of Applejack's very big lie.

A young Big Mac and Applejack are walking in Ponyville, arguing over who would run Sweet Apple Acres better, she or him. They bump into Filthy Rich and his fiancée, Spoiled Milk, who tell them about how close both families have been for a very long time. Filthy Rich tells them that he wants to sell the Apple family's cider at Rich Barnyard Bargains, the store he inherited from his father. Applejack quickly agrees, but Big Mac says there's no way Granny Smith would allow that. Applejack makes the deal with Filthy Rich anyway, but finds out Granny Smith will not allow the Rich family to sell Apple family cider. This starts a cascade of lies from Applejack. When one crazy lie leads to another and they all end up at the hospital with Granny almost sawing off Big Mac's leg, Applejack confesses to it all.

Big Mac actually takes some of the blame for talking more than listening, so he and Applejack make up. Granny Smith also forgives her, but she says she is sure she'll be in charge of the farm for a *loooong* time now. And she warns Filthy Rich not to retaliate or she'll let his grandfather know. In present time, Apple Bloom is a little relieved to learn she is not the only one who has lied in their family. Though Applejack isn't proud of her behavior, she believes it taught her a big lesson on how important honesty is.

Friendship Lesson:

"NOPONY STARTS OUT PERFECT, AND SOMETIMES YOU GOTTA MAKE A FEW MISTAKES TO FIGURE OUT WHO YOU ARE." —APPLE BLOOM

Top Bolt

Rainbow Dash is excited to have some time off from the Wonderbolts Academy when the Cutie Map sends both her and Twilight Sparkle back there. They figure out quickly their friendship problem involves an overconfident pony named Sky Stinger and his best friend, a much less confident pony named Vapor Trail. The two have always flown together, but Rainbow Dash and Twilight soon realize that Vapor has been using her wings to increase Sky Stinger's flight power. And because she is so focused on making him look good, Vapor can't spend any time improving her own skills. When it comes time to do the solo testing, they both are going to suffer, and so might their friendship.

Twilight and Rainbow Dash disagree on how to handle

this. Twilight thinks they should come out and tell Sky Stinger the truth, but Rainbow Dash thinks it will undermine his confidence and he'll fail. Rainbow Dash and Twilight decide to work with both ponies individually to try to improve their skills and see if they can fix their flying issues that way. But Sky Stinger isn't trying very hard because of his overconfidence. Finally, Vapor admits to Sky that she's been helping him the whole time. He lashes out in anger, breaking her heart. Twilight now thinks Rainbow Dash was right the whole time and they should have done things her way.

Twilight approaches Sky Stinger and convinces him that trying hard is something everypony has to do, no matter how much natural talent you have. Even she, the Princess of Friendship, had to work on being a good friend! And Rainbow Dash convinces Vapor that if she just had the confidence to come out of Sky Stinger's shadow, she could learn many new tricks. Both fliers come together and apologize. They work together to help each other improve, and they both are accepted into the Wonderbolts Academy. As they fly off together, Twilight and Rainbow Dash's cutie marks start to glow, meaning their friendship mission was a success!

Friendship Lesson:

"REAL FRIENDS DON'T TRY TO STEAL YOUR SPOTLIGHT. THEY HELP YOU GET BETTER SO YOU CAN SHINE BRIGHT AND BE THE BEST PONY YOU CAN BE!" —TWILIGHT SPARKLE

To Where and Back Again: Part 1

Starlight Glimmer is very nervous because she has been invited back to her old village for the Sunset Festival. While she is happy they invited her, she is plagued by bad dreams that the villages will all reject her when she gets there, not having truly forgiven her. Her friends in Ponyville encourage her, telling her that she has changed immeasurably and everypony will see that. She agrees reluctantly and brings Trixie with her for comfort.

She attends the festival and finds the ponies there all

treat her very well. But she gets quickly overwhelmed with the attention, and she and Trixie race back home to Ponyville early. When they get there, they find that all the important ponies in both Ponyville and Canterlot have been replaced by Changelings! Trixie has no idea to handle a situation like this, and when Thorax comes to tell them about the ponies in the Crystal Empire, he admits he has no idea, either.

Trixie, Thorax, and Starlight stare at one another in horror, realizing there is nopony with enough magic to help them. But just then Discord magically appears. After making completely certain that he isn't a Changeling, they tell him about the situation. Furious that anyone has hurt his precious Fluttershy, he transports them to the outskirts of the Changeling Kingdom, home of Queen Chrysalis. The unlikely quartet is the only hope to save Equestria....

To Where and Back Again: Part 2

Once arriving on the outskirts of the Changeling Kingdom, Thorax informs the group that Queen Chrysalis's throne is carved from an ancient dark stone and it soaks up all non-Changeling magic, rendering Starlight Glimmer, Trixie, Thorax, and Discord all powerless.

Everyone turns to Starlight for her leadership. She tells them they must infiltrate the hive and destroy the throne. The group gets to Chrysalis's throne room and discovers all their friends trapped in cocoons on the ceiling. Chrysalis laughs, saying she didn't think Starlight was important enough to capture at first, but it *was* part of her plan to have her and Trixie show up! However, the queen quickly realizes she has not been looking at Trixie, but Thorax. Starlight tells Chrysalis that she and her Changelings don't have to battle like this! She tells the queen that ever since Thorax made friends and started sharing love, he hasn't needed to feed as often as Changelings usually do. By giving love, he is getting love back. The other Changelings start to believe her, but Chrysalis won't hear any of it. Ignoring Starlight's words, Chrysalis starts to drain the love out of Thorax. He is unable to hold on to the love inside him, so Starlight tells him to just share it. This creates a burst of light that blows away Chrysalis and transforms Thorax into a new form of Changeling! The other Changelings do this as well and their bodies are also transformed. All this magic causes Chrysalis's throne to explode, and the ponies who the Changelings captured are freed.

Everypony is grateful to Starlight and congratulates her on her fine leadership. She tries to offer Chrysalis her hoof in friendship, but Chrysalis rejects her and swears revenge before flying away. Thorax is appointed the Changelings' new ruler and Equestria is saved! Starlight has learned that she can be both a true friend and a strong leader.

Friendship Lesson:

"A REAL LEADER DOESN'T FORCE HER SUBJECTS TO DENY WHO THEY ARE! SHE CELEBRATES WHAT MAKES THEM UNIQUE AND LISTENS WHEN ONE OF THEM FINDS A BETTER WAY!" —STARLIGHT GLIMMER

SONG LYRICS

DJ PON-3 is Equestria's hottest musical act! What's her real name? Nopony knows. She's mysterious like that. Got an event that needs a few jams? DJ Pon-3 has a turntable! She can spin all night long and never break a sweat. Check out some of the tracks she's got, ready to go!

Song: "Hearts as Strong as Horses"
Episode: "Flight to the Finish"
Lyrics by Ed Valentine & D. Ingram
Music by Daniel Ingram

CUTIE MARK CRUSADERS
We're the toughest little ponies in town....
Got the moves, got the mojo....
No harder-working ponies around....
We are a trio, work as a team....
We'll be the first ponies out on the flag-waving scene....

We get going when the going get tough!
We know our very best is just
never enough
We're kinda short, but so what?
We don't get defeated....
We could take a little break, but we don't need it....

We've got hearts
as strong as horses!
We've got hearts
as strong as horses!

We've got hearts....
Hearts strong as horses!

When we put our minds together,
we can achieve....
We're the Cutie Mark Crusaders,
and you should believe
we've got determination
to represent the nation
for the win!

We've got hearts
as strong as horses!
We've got hearts
as strong as horses!
We've got hearts
as strong as horses!
And we're playing to win....
as we gallop to glory....
We can conquer any challenge
we're in....

We've got hearts....
Hearts strong as horses!
Hearts strong as horses!

Song: "Apples to the Core"
Episode: "Pinkie Apple Pie"
Lyrics by Natasha Levinger &
Daniel Ingram
Music by Daniel Ingram

APPLEJACK, APPLE BLOOM, BIG MAC, GRANNY SMITH
We've traveled the road of generations
joined by a common bond.
We sing our song 'cross the pony nation
from Equestria and beyond....

APPLEJACK & APPLE BLOOM
We're Apples forever,
Apples together....
We're fam'ly but so much more....
No matter what comes, we will face the
weather....
We're Apples to the core!

BIG MAC
Eyup!

APPLE BLOOM
There's no place that I'd rather be
than traveling with my family....
Friends all around come to join and see
as we sing out across the land!

APPLEJACK, APPLE BLOOM, BIG MAC, GRANNY SMITH
We're Apples forever,
Apples together....
We're fam'ly but so much more....
No matter what comes, we will face the
weather....
We're Apples to the core!

GRANNY SMITH
We're peas in a pod; we're think as thieves—
any cliché you can throw at me!
We're here for each other through thick
and thin....
You're always welcome with your
Apple kin!

PINKIE PIE
You're more fun than the color pink
or balloons flying over your fav'rite drink....
The love I feel here is swim not sink
as we party across this land!

EVERYPONY
We're Apples forever,
Apples together....
We're fam'ly but so much more....
No matter what comes, we will face the
weather....
We're Apples to the core!

Song: "The Superduper Party Pony"
Episode: "Pinkie Pride"
Lyrics by Amy Keating Rogers & D. Ingram
Music by Daniel Ingram

CHEESE SANDWICH
The superduper party pony—that pony is me,
I always knew that was the kind of pony I
would be!

PINKIE PIE
Me too!

CHEESE SANDWICH
Come on, ponies, who here likes to party?!
Haha, you do; I can tell!
When I was but a little colt I just wanted to
play....

PINKIE PIE
Like me!

CHEESE SANDWICH
But everypony told me, "Cheese, that fun just
wastes the day!"

PINKIE PIE
As if!

CHEESE SANDWICH
But when I threw a party, and I busted out
some moves....

PINKIE PIE
Uh-huh!

CHEESE SANDWICH
The ponies fin'ly saw the light and got into
the groove!

PINKIE PIE
You know it!

CHEESE SANDWICH
The superduper party pony—that pony is me

PINKIE PIE
And me!

CHEESE SANDWICH
You'll never meet another party pony quite
like Cheese!

PINKIE PIE
Uh, Pinkie?

CHEESE SANDWICH
Hey, good-lookin'! Want some mayonnaise?
My parties are all off the hook,
I never plan them by the book....
They start out fun then—whoopsidaisy—
Everypony just gets crazy!
Bored of snacks made by your mom?
How 'bout a giant party bomb!
Huge pinanta filled with cake or
dive into my fruit-punch lake!

EXTRA PONY
Geronimo!

CHEESE SANDWICH
The superduper party pony—that pony is me
You'll never meet another party pony
quite like
Cheeeese!
Come on, kid, take it for a spin!

EXTRA PONY
Golly! Thanks, Mister!

CHEESE SANDWICH
Oh, when I throw a Cheese party, be sure not
to be lame,
and miss my pie fights, wacky kites, and
streamers in your mane....

Fizzy drinks, Hawaiian shirts, and Brie
fondue delight....
You know that with Cheese Sandwich, you'll
be partying all night

RAINBOW DASH

Come on, everypony. Let's party down with
Cheese!

FLUTTERSHY

You're really a certified party pony?

CHEESE SANDWICH

That's right; that's my guarantee!
The superduper party pony—that pony
is me!

PINKIE PIE

But what about the super
party pony named Pinkie?

CHEESE SANDWICH

Aw, thanks, buddy—you're
going to love this party!
Hey, kid, have a streamer...
on me!

Song: "The Pony I Want to Be"
Episode: "Crusaders of the Lost Mark"
Lyrics by Daniel Ingram &
Amy Keating Rogers
Music by Daniel Ingram

DIAMOND TIARA

If I'm a diamond then why do I feel so rough?
I'm as strong as a stone, even that's not
enough....
There's something jagged in me,
and I've made such mistakes.
I thought that diamonds were hard, though I
feel I could break.

Would you believe that I've always wished I
could be somepony else,

yet I can't see what I need to do to be the
pony I want to be?

I've been told my whole life what to do, what
to say....
No pony showed me that there might be
some better way....
And now I feel like I'm lost; I don't know
what to do....
The ground is sinking away; I'm about to fall
through....

Would you believe that I've always wished I
could be somepony else,
yet I can't see What I need to do to be the
pony I want to be?
To be the pony I want to be....

Song: "I'll Fly (to the End of the Sky)"
Episode: "Tanks for the Memories"
Lyrics by Daniel Ingram &
Amy Keating Rogers
Music by Daniel Ingram

RAINBOW DASH
When life gives you lemons,
you can make lemonade....
But life gave me Tank here,
and my choice has long been made.
No winter will come to Ponyville....
I'll do it on my own....
I will keep you by my side so I will not
be alone.

And I'll fly and I'll fly until the end of the sky
so I'll be the one who doesn't
have to say good-bye.
I'll clear the skies forever....
So we won't be apart.
I'll keep the weather warm for you, and the
winter will never start!

Weather-makers, Pegasi,
you make the seasons in the sky....
I don't want to sabotage you
but, you see, I've got to try....
No winter can come here now....
I'll keep the warmth and the sun somehow....
I'm sorry, ponies; this has to be
for I need my friend and he needs me!
I know it's wrong, but what does it matter
'cause nothing's gonna stop me now....
I'll change it all....
It's only the weather, and no ponies gonna
bring me down!
I'll keep the sunlight shining free!
And I'll bust the clouds apart so you can stay
with me!

And I'll fly and I'll fly until the end of the sky
so I'll be the one who doesn't
have to say good-bye.
I'll clear the skies forever....
So we won't be apart.
I'll keep the weather warm for you and the
winter will never start!

Song: "Let the Rainbow Remind You"
Episode: "Twilight's Kingdom—Part 2"
**Lyrics by Meghan McCarthy &
Daniel Ingram
Music by Daniel Ingram**

TWILIGHT
Each one of us has something special
that makes us different,
that makes us rare.

FLUTTERSHY
We have a light that shines within us
that we were always meant to share.

MANE SIX
And when we come together,

combine the light that shines within
there is nothing we can't do.
There is no battle we can't win....
When we come together....

There'll be a star to guide the way;
It's inside us every day.
See it now.
See it now.
Let the rainbow remind you that
together we will always shine.
Let the rainbow remind you that forever
this will be our time.

TWILIGHT
Let the rainbow remind you that
together we will always shine.

Song: "The Magic Inside"
Episode: "The Mane Attraction"
**Lyrics by Daniel Ingram &
Amy Keating Rogers
Music by Daniel Ingram**

COUNTESS COLORATURA
I'm here to show you who I am....
Throw off the veil, it's fin'ly time....
There's more to me than glitz and glam,
oh-woah....
And now I feel my stars align....
For I had believed what I was sold;
I did all the things that I was told,
but all that has changed, and now I'm bold
'cause I know...

That I am just a pony...
I make mistakes from time to time....
But now I know the real me
and put my heart out on the line,
And let the magic in my heart stay true.
Oh-whoa-whoa-whoa-whoa.
And let the magic in my heart stay true.

Oh-whoa-whoa-whoa-whoa...
just like the magic inside of you.

And now I see those colors right before
my eyes.
I hear my voice so clearly, and I know that it
is right....
I thought I was weak, but I am strong...
They sold me the world, but they were
wrong...
And now that I'm back, I still belong 'cause
I know...

That I am just a pony...
I make mistakes from time to time....
But now I know the real me
And put my heart out on the line,
And let the magic in my heart stay true.
Oh-whoa-whoa-whoa-whoa.
And let the magic in my heart stay true.
Oh-whoa-whoa-whoa-whoa...
just like the magic inside of you.
Just like the magic inside of you.

Song: "Can I Do It On My Own?"
Episode: "Fluter Brutter"
Lyrics by Meghan McCarthy, Dave Rapp &
Daniel Ingram
Music by Daniel Ingram

FLUTTERSHY
Everypony has times in their lives
when their hearts are filled with doubt.

ZEPHYR BREEZE
Frustration builds up inside,
and it makes you want to shout!

RAINBOW DASH
But if you just take that first step,
the next one will appear

RAINBOW DASH & FLUTTERSHY
And you find you can walk, then run,
then fly...
into the stratosphere.

You've got to give it your best so you can pass
the test.
Give it everything that you've got....
And we know you can win you just have to
begin....
Have to give it your very best shot.

ZEPHYR BREEZE
There are times when you want to give up,
when you think that you can't go on....

RAINBOW DASH & FLUTTERSHY
But if you fight through with all of your
might,
you will find that you can't go wrong....
That you could do it all along!

FLUTTERSHY
Everypony has times in their lives
when their hearts are filled with doubt.

RAINBOW DASH
But if you just give it your all,
you'll start to work it out.

ZEPHYR BREEZE
And I know I can't give in too soon...
Get myself in the zone,
And I find I can walk, then run...

EVERYPONY
Then fly....

ZEPHYR BREEZE
And I can do it on my own!

RAINBOW DASH & FLUTTERSHY
You can do it on your own!

ZEPHYR BREEZE
I can do it on my own!
I can do it on my own!

Song: "Out On My Own"
Episode: "On Your Marks"
Lyrics by Daniel Ingram, Dave Polsky, and Josh Haber
Music by Daniel Ingram

APPLE BLOOM

I never imagined myself out on my own—
Tryin' to find out what's next for me.
The Cutie Mark Crusaders have always been my home.
Maybe now there's more that I could be...

I guess as time goes by
everypony has to go out on their own.
And maybe someday I'll have to try
something new that's just for me.
A little something that could be
just my own and I won't feel so left behind.

We used to say that we'd be always side by side.
But maybe things are changin' and this could mean good-bye.
We've always been crusadin'—what else is there for me.

I guess as time goes by
everypony has to go out on their own.
And maybe someday I'll have to try
something new that's just for me.
A little something that could be
just my own and I won't feel
so left behind.

Song: "A Changeling Can Change"
Episode: "The Times They Are a Changling!"
Lyrics by Kevin Burke & Chris Wyatt
Music by Daniel Ingram

SPIKE

Would you say I'm a hero, glorious and brave,
if I told you something you wouldn't believe?
That sometimes I'm scared...
And I can make mistakes, and I'm not so heroic, it seems.
But if day can turn to night and the darkness turns to light,
then why can't we imagine
a Changling can change?

No two ponies are exactly the same...
No two snowflakes ever match their design...
And I thought I was strong, but I was nothing but wrong

when I forgot to be friendly and kind
But if day and turn to night and the darkness turn to light,
then why can't we imagine
a Changeling can change?

Would you say I'm a hero, glorious and brave,
if I told you something you wouldn't believe?
This changeling, it seems, knows the real me
And would stay by my side till the end!
So if day and turn to night and the darkness turn to light,
then why can't we imagine...
Just why can't we imagine?
Then why can't we imagine
a Changeling can change?

239

SCRAPBOOK

DEAR CHEESE SANDWICH,
I HAD SO MUCH FUN AT THE
PARTY! THANK YOU FOR INVITING
ME. YOU'RE VERY TALENTED. MY
FAVORITE SONG WAS "LET THE GOOD
TIMES FOAL"—SO FUNNY! PLEASE
KEEP IN TOUCH.
—FLUTTERSHY

Party on!
—Cheese Sandwich

Hey, Rainbow Dash,
I'm really diggin' your whole vibe.
The hair, the colors...it's totally
groovy. Let's hang sometime. You,
me, and Zecora can read each
other's auras. Keep in touch.
Blessings,

Tree Hugger

TO OCTAVIA—
I HAD A DREAM ABOUT YOU!
YOUR CELLO WAS BEAUTIFUL!
—SWEETIE BELLE

To Moondancer—
Hey! It's been a while since I've seen you. I hope everything is going well. I know you like to spend time alone, but being around other ponies is good for your spirit. Come say hello soon. I miss you.
—Twilight Sparkle

Sequin & Sashes
4-EVER!
—Sassy Saddles

Cherry Jubilee—
I know you think cherries are the best, but hear me out. Apples are really stinkin' good! You can make pies, turnovers, and even SAUCE out of 'em. I'm tellin' you, you're doin' it all wrong. Give apples a chance!

—Applejack

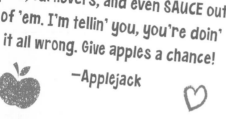

Hi, Claude,

Can you please let me know when the special puppet I ordered will be ready? I need it for a big event. It's very important. Please, will you let me know?

Thanks!
—Rarity

PUPPETS TAKE TIME!
Be patient.
—Claude